GUARDED HEARTS

A SWEETGUM MEADOWS ROMANCE BOOK 12

IMANI PRICE

Copyright © 2025 by Imani Price
www.ImaniPrice.com

First Edition: November 2025

ISBN 979-8-89283-312-7 (ebook)
ISBN 979-8-89283-313-4 (paperback)

Published by Books to Hook Publishing, LLC.
www.BooksToHook.com

CONTENTS

CHAPTER ONE

The note was folded into a hard little square at the bottom of Omari's backpack. Naomi smoothed it on the kitchen counter with damp fingers while pasta water hissed and popped. Three cramped, shaky words stared up at her:

Go back home.

Naomi's hand stilled on the paper. The same hand that had shelved picture books at Sweetgum Elementary for three years, that had guided small fingers across story pages, that had waved to other mothers at pickup—that hand now trembled against cheap notebook paper torn at the edges.

At the table, Omari hunched over his math worksheet like he was protecting state secrets. His pencil—the mechanical one with the good eraser that didn't smudge—tap-tap-tapped against the page. His shoulders sat bunched up near his ears.

"Baby, where did you get this?" She kept her voice soft, the same tone she used when kids came to the library crying about lost books.

"My locker." He didn't look up. The pencil kept tapping.

"Today?"

He nodded once, sharp and quick.

"Was it Marcus and Devin again?"

Another nod. He pressed the eraser to the paper and left it there, like pressure could hold everything still.

Her phone buzzed against the counter: *Andre*. The preview showed enough:

> We need to discuss Omari's future. This can't wait.

She knew better. Andre's version of "discussing their son" usually meant lecturing her about her choices while fishing for information he could use later. She flipped the phone face-down and turned off the burner with more force than necessary.

The silence stretched. Outside, Mrs. Patterson's dog started his evening bark-fest at absolutely nothing. The refrigerator hummed. Omari's pencil went *tap-tap-tap* like a heartbeat that wouldn't slow down.

"Tomorrow morning," Naomi said, sliding into the chair beside him, close enough to smell the lotion she still smoothed through his hair each night, "I'm meeting with Mrs. Corbin. Not as Ms. Ellis from the library. As your mama."

He stopped tapping.

"Something has to change, baby. I don't know what yet, but we're going to figure it out together."

He chewed his bottom lip, the way he did when thinking hard. "Are you going to tell them to stop?"

The question broke her heart. As if telling bullies to stop had ever worked in the history of elementary schools.

"I'm going to make sure they can't get to you," she said instead. "Whatever that takes."

~

SWEETGUM ELEMENTARY'S front office smelled like copy toner and the coffee Mrs. Henderson brewed too strong every morning. At 8:15, Naomi sat in the visitor chair across from Mrs. Corbin's desk. The same chair she'd sat in ten years ago when her mother came to advocate for her. The staff chair on the other side stayed empty—she'd made sure of that.

"Naomi." Mrs. Corbin folded her manicured hands. "I want to be clear about boundaries. In this office, you're Omari's mother first. Period."

Naomi pulled out her composition notebook—the one with the bright floral cover. "I'm listening."

"Effective immediately: new locker assignment in Bay C, away from Marcus and Devin. For the next five days, supervised lunch seating. Mrs. Rivera will meet with Omari tomorrow for conflict resolution strategies." Mrs. Corbin's voice was crisp, businesslike. "All communication goes through the parent portal, not your staff email. Clean paper trail."

Naomi wrote it all down in her careful teacher handwriting, the same script she'd used for lesson plans. But her heart was hammering like she was sixteen again, sitting in this same building, feeling small.

"What about recess?" she asked. "PE? The hallways between classes?"

"We'll monitor more closely. But Naomi..." Mrs. Corbin's voice softened slightly. "You know as well as I do that we can't be everywhere. Sometimes the best defense is teaching kids how to handle these situations themselves."

The words hit like a slap. *Teach him to handle it himself.* As if her ten-year-old son should have to learn how to fight his own battles because the adults couldn't protect him.

"Understood." Naomi closed the notebook. Today she wasn't Ms. Ellis who organized the book fair and knew every child's reading level. She was just another mother who'd been told her child's safety was ultimately his own responsibility.

Back in the children's library, she straightened the easy readers with mechanical precision. *Frog and Toad*, *Henry and Mudge*, all the reliable friends marching in neat rows. A group of second-graders tumbled in for story time, and she painted on her librarian smile.

"Who wants to hear about a mouse with a cookie?"

They cheered. She read with voices and gestures, lost herself in the rhythm of call-and-response, the way the children leaned forward during the good parts. For thirty minutes, the world was simple again.

But between read-alouds and shelf-straightening, Mrs. Corbin's words echoed: *Sometimes the best defense is teaching kids how to handle these situations themselves.*

At 3:10, she hung her staff badge on its hook beside her computer and signed out like everyone else. The weight of it—being just another parent with just another problem—sat heavy on her shoulders.

PINE STREET STRETCHED AHEAD of them, afternoon light slanting gold across shop windows. The bakery's door was propped open, releasing the warm smell of dinner rolls. Justin Time's Clock and Watch Repair glowed with its single lamp, and she could see Justin bent over a workbench through the window.

"Where are we going?" Omari asked, kicking at a pebble.

"I want to check something out," she said. They'd passed the sign dozens of times: *Sweetgum Jiu-Jitsu & Wellness* in clean black letters on large front windows. She'd never paid it much attention before today.

"What kind of something?"

She paused at the window, peering through the glass. Soft gray mats covered most of the floor, and neat rows of white uniforms hung from wooden pegs. A man was demonstrating something to a small group of kids—showing them how to fall backward and roll up again, safe and controlled.

"Maybe something that could help," she said.

The bell chimed when they stepped inside. Everything was clean lines and warm light—the kind of space that made you stand a little straighter without trying.

"Hi there!" The woman behind the desk bounded up with a smile that lit her whole face. Purple belt around her waist, bright yellow headband holding back hair twisted into perfect spirals. "I'm Kiana. Can I help you?"

"I'm Naomi Ellis. This is Omari. We were just..." She trailed off. *Just what? Just desperate? Just out of options?*

"Just curious," she finished.

"Absolutely! Are you thinking about classes for him, or—"

"Mom, look." Omari had wandered closer to the mats, where the man was still working with the kids. "They're learning how to fall without getting hurt."

The man looked up at Omari's voice, and Naomi's breath caught in her throat like a door slamming.

Khadir Grant.

Seventeen years fell away in an instant. She was back in AP History, watching him fix the wobbly library table with an index card and electrical tape, never making a show of it. The boy who'd walked her to her car after the homecoming dance because her date had been too drunk to drive, who'd waited until she was safely inside before heading to his own beat-up Honda.

His shoulders were broader now, his movements sure and economical. But his eyes—warm brown eyes that noticed everything and judged nothing—those were exactly the same.

"Khadir," Kiana called. "We have some visitors."

He said something quiet to the kids that made them giggle, then stood and walked over. Recognition flickered across his face like a match striking, followed by a real smile—slow, genuine, and entirely focused on her.

"Naomi Ellis." He said it like her name was something he'd been keeping safe. "I wondered if you'd ever come back to Sweetgum."

"I never left," she said, then immediately felt foolish. Of course he'd know that. In a town this small, everyone knew everyone else's business.

"Good to see you," he said, and his voice was deeper now, seasoned. He looked at Omari, who was still watching the kids on the mat. "You too, young man. You like what you're seeing over there?"

Omari nodded, suddenly shy.

"Want to try it?"

"Try what?"

"Learning how to fall without getting hurt." Khadir's tone was easy, no pressure. "It's the first thing we teach. Shoes off, step onto the mat, and I'll show you."

Naomi started to say they were just looking, but something in Khadir's expression stopped her. He was watching Omari with the same careful attention he'd given to that wobbly table all those years ago—like here was a problem that deserved his full focus.

"Can I, Mom?"

She found herself nodding.

Khadir showed Omari where to put his shoes, how to use the hand sanitizer, how to bow when stepping onto the mat. "It's how we say thank you," he explained. "To the space and to each other."

"First thing we teach is the break-fall," he said, settling onto the mat. "That's falling safe on purpose. Chin tucked, arms crossed to protect yourself, and then—"

He demonstrated, curling back with his chin to his chest,

then slapping the mat with his palms in a controlled *thump*. He rolled up to sitting in one smooth motion.

"Bodies remember what we teach them," he said, eyes on Omari. "Want to try?"

Under Khadir's patient guidance, Omari crossed his arms over his chest, tucked his chin, and let himself fall back. When his hands hit the mat, the sound was softer than Khadir's but just as controlled. He popped up with surprise written all over his face.

"That felt..." He paused, searching for words. "Safe."

"That's the point," Khadir said. "If you know how to fall safely, you're not afraid of falling. And if you're not afraid of falling, you can try things. Take risks. Stand up to challenges."

Naomi's chest tightened. *Stand up to challenges.* Like bullies who left notes in lockers.

"We also teach how to get back up with intention," Khadir continued. "Not scrambling, not panicked. Step by step, on purpose. Want to see?"

He showed Omari the technical stand-up—how to post one hand, bring one foot up, rise with control and balance. Omari tried it, wobbly at first, then smoother.

"Excellent," Khadir said, and the pride in his voice was unmistakable. "You're a natural."

Across the room, other parents were watching their kids practice the same movements. Normal parents with normal problems, Naomi thought. Not parents whose ex-husbands sent manipulative messages or whose children found hate notes in their lockers.

"Mrs. Ellis?" Khadir was beside her now, voice pitched low so Omari couldn't hear. "Can I ask what brought you in today?"

The question was gentle, but something in his tone said he already suspected the answer. In a town like Sweetgum, word traveled fast. The school meeting this morning, the way she'd looked when she walked in—he was putting pieces together.

"Just..." She gestured vaguely toward Omari, who was practicing his stand-up. "Looking for options."

His eyes held hers for a long moment. "Kids who know how to fall safely and get up with purpose—they walk differently. Carry themselves differently. Bullies notice that."

The word hung in the air between them. *Bullies.* He'd said it so she didn't have to.

"How much do classes cost?" The question came out sharper than she'd intended.

"For kids like Omari? We'll figure something out." His tone was matter-of-fact. "But I'm not just talking about him."

"What do you mean?"

"Confidence is contagious," he said. "When a child sees their parent learning something new, taking up space, getting stronger—it changes how they see themselves. How they move through the world."

She looked at him sharply. "Are you suggesting—"

"I'm suggesting that maybe you both could benefit from learning how to fall safely and get back up on purpose." His smile was gentle but knowing. "First class is always free. For both of you."

"I don't think—"

"Mom?" Omari appeared at her elbow, slightly breathless and glowing with something she hadn't seen in weeks. "Can we come back?"

She looked at her son—really looked at him. His shoulders had dropped back down where they belonged. The tight line of his mouth had relaxed. For the first time in days, he looked like a kid instead of a small soldier braced for battle.

"What do you think?" Khadir asked quietly. "Are you ready to learn how to fall without getting hurt?"

The way he said it made it sound like more than just a martial arts technique. Like he was offering them both something they desperately needed—a way to feel steady in an unsteady world.

Her phone buzzed in her pocket. Another message from Andre, no doubt. But for the first time in months, she didn't feel the familiar clench of anxiety at the sound.

"When's the next class?" she heard herself ask.

"Tomorrow at four," Kiana called from the front desk, where she'd apparently been listening. "Ghee rental is included."

"Ghee?"

"The uniform," Khadir explained. "Though you can start in regular workout clothes if you prefer."

"What do I need to know?"

"Nothing," he said. "Just show up ready to learn. Everything else, we'll teach you."

Omari was practically bouncing on his toes. "Really? We can both come?"

"If your mom wants to," Khadir said, but his eyes were on Naomi, warm and encouraging and somehow protective. Like he understood that this decision was about more than just martial arts classes. Like he knew she needed someone in her corner.

"Yes," she said, and the word felt like stepping off a cliff. "We'll both come."

"Perfect." He handed her a card with the studio's information. "See you tomorrow at four."

As they walked back to the car, Omari chattered about break-falls and technical stand-ups, his whole body animated in a way she hadn't seen since before the bullying started.

"Mom?" he said as they reached their car. "Do you think I'll be braver now?"

The question stopped her cold. Not stronger, not tougher. *Braver.*

"I think," she said carefully, "that you're already braver than you know. But maybe now you'll feel it too."

He smiled—the first real smile she'd seen in weeks—and climbed into the backseat.

As she started the car, her phone buzzed again. Andre's name flashed on the screen, but for once, the sight of it didn't make her stomach clench. Tomorrow she was going to learn how to fall without getting hurt. How to get back up on purpose.

Maybe that would be enough to handle whatever Andre thought he needed to "discuss."

But somehow, thinking about the way Khadir had looked at her—steady, knowing, protective—she suspected it might be enough to handle a lot more than that.

CHAPTER TWO

The last student bowed off the mat at seven-thirty, and Khadir finally allowed himself to breathe. The dojo settled into its evening quiet—just the hum of the air purifier and the distant sound of Kiana closing out the register at the front desk.

"Good class tonight," she called, not looking up from her paperwork. "That new kid, Tyler, is really coming along."

Khadir nodded, rolling up the mats they'd used for partner work. But his mind wasn't on Tyler or any of the other students. It kept circling back to the moment Naomi Ellis had walked through his door, looking like she was carrying the weight of the world and trying not to let it show.

Naomi Ellis. Even thinking her name sent something warm and complicated through his chest.

Seventeen years. Seventeen years since he'd watched her debate their AP History teacher about Reconstruction era policies until Mr. Peterson finally admitted she had a point. Seventeen years since he'd fixed that wobbly library table with an index card and watched her smile like he'd just solved world hunger. Seventeen years since homecoming night, when Derek

Matthews had been too drunk to drive and Khadir had walked her to her car instead, wishing the ten-minute trip could last forever.

She'd married someone else six months later. Andre Pierce, who'd been everything Khadir wasn't—loud, confident, quarterback of the football team. The kind of guy who never had to wonder if he was good enough, because everyone already told him he was.

Khadir had enlisted two weeks after their wedding.

"You planning to stand there all night?" Kiana's voice broke through his thoughts. She was leaning against the doorframe, keys jingling in her hand. "Because I've got a date with some leftover Chinese food and a Netflix documentary."

"Sorry." He shook his head, focusing on the present. "Just thinking."

"About the Ellis family?"

He paused in his mat-rolling. "How did you—"

"Please. I've been working here for three years. I know your 'I'm trying not to get invested' face." She grinned. "Plus, the way you looked at her? Like you'd seen a ghost and won the lottery at the same time."

Heat climbed up his neck. "It's not—"

"Relax, boss. Your secret's safe with me." Kiana's expression grew more serious. "Though I have to say, that little boy looked like he needed exactly what we offer here. And his mama... well, she looked like she could use some peace of mind."

Peace of mind. That was one way to put it. From what Khadir had observed during their brief visit, Naomi was running on empty—all sharp edges and barely contained worry. The kind of exhaustion that came from fighting battles on too many fronts.

"What do you know about the situation?" he asked, trying to keep his voice casual.

Kiana shrugged. "Just what everyone knows. Messy divorce a couple years back. Andre Pierce never did learn how to take no for an answer, even when they were married. Word is he's been making her life difficult ever since she moved back."

Khadir's hands stilled on the mat. "Making her life difficult how?"

"Nothing concrete. Just... you know how it is in a town this size. People notice things. Like how she always looks tired at the school pickup. How she keeps to herself more than she used to. How her ex seems to show up places she's going to be, even though they're divorced."

The knot in Khadir's stomach tightened. He'd opened the dojo with a simple mission: teach people how to protect themselves, how to move through the world with confidence and peace. But sometimes protection meant more than just physical techniques.

"Think they'll come to class tomorrow?" Kiana asked.

"I hope so." The words came out quieter than he'd intended.

"You planning to partner with her?"

Khadir looked up sharply. "What's that supposed to mean?"

"Nothing bad. Just..." Kiana tilted her head, studying him. "You had that look again. The one that says you're already planning how to help."

She wasn't wrong. He'd spent the better part of the evening thinking about training progressions for Naomi—how to build her confidence without overwhelming her, how to teach her spatial awareness and boundary-setting in ways that wouldn't feel scary. How to give her tools she could use both on and off the mat.

"I was thinking you could work with Omari," he said. "He seems to respond well to you."

"And you work with his mama."

"It makes sense from a teaching perspective—"

"Uh-huh." Kiana's grin was knowing. "Sure it does."

Khadir finished rolling the mat and stored it in the closet, buying himself time to think. The truth was, he did want to work with Naomi. But not for the reasons Kiana was implying.

Well, not entirely for those reasons.

"There's a rule," he said finally. "One I made when I opened this place."

"What kind of rule?"

"Don't compete off the mat." He straightened, meeting her eyes. "The dojo is about growth, about building people up. It's not about winning or losing or... or trying to prove anything to anyone."

"And working with Naomi Ellis would be competing how, exactly?"

The question hung in the air between them. How could he explain that being around Naomi felt like stepping into a sparring match he'd lost seventeen years ago? That seeing her again brought back all the old feelings of not being enough, not being the kind of man someone like her would choose?

"I don't know," he admitted. "But I know I want to help her. And I know that wanting to help someone and wanting something from them can get tangled up in ways that aren't fair to anyone."

Kiana was quiet for a long moment, studying his face. "You know what I think?"

"I'm sure you're going to tell me."

"I think maybe the rule about not competing off the mat works both ways. Maybe it also means not competing with yourself. Not letting old fears keep you from doing what's right."

She grabbed her purse from behind the desk and headed for the door. "Lock up when you're ready. And Khadir? That little boy needs someone who sees him. Really sees him. And his mama needs someone who understands that protecting people isn't about winning—it's about showing up."

The door chimed as she left, and Khadir was alone with his thoughts.

He finished his closing routine—checking the locks, turning off the lights, setting the alarm. But instead of heading home, he found himself walking down Pine Street toward Roasted Beans Coffee Spot. The place stayed open until nine, and he had a sudden need for Joanne's mint tea and a few minutes to clear his head.

The coffee shop was nearly empty when he walked in, just a couple of college students hunched over textbooks in the corner and Mrs. Zhang from Sweet and Spicy Chinese Palace reading a paperback romance near the window.

"Khadir!" Joanne looked up from wiping down the espresso machine. "Let me guess—mint tea to go?"

"Actually, I'll stay for a bit tonight. And I was wondering if you had any bulletin board space."

"Depends what you're advertising." She poured hot water over a tea bag and slid the mug across the counter. "Please tell me you're not trying to recruit people for one of those mixed martial arts cage fighting things."

"Confidence and self-defense classes," he said, pulling a folded flyer from his pocket. "Nothing fancy. Just basic skills for people who want to feel steadier in the world."

Joanne studied the flyer, which featured a simple design with the dojo's logo and information about beginner-friendly classes. No intimidating photos of people in fighting stances, no promises about learning to "destroy your enemies." Just clean, professional information about building confidence and learning practical skills.

"I like it," she said, pinning it to the community board near the entrance. "We get a lot of parents in here who worry about their kids getting picked on. This might be exactly what they need."

"That's the idea."

He settled into a chair by the window with his tea, watching the evening foot traffic on Pine Street. A few storefronts down, the lights were still on in Sweet and Spicy Chinese Palace. Mrs. Zhang must have seen him looking, because she waved from her seat by the window.

Mrs. Zhang. An idea began forming in his mind.

He'd been thinking about organizing a community event—something to introduce more families to the dojo's approach to self-defense. Not a demonstration of techniques, but something gentler. A way for parents and kids to see that martial arts could be about more than fighting.

Maybe a "Confidence and Kindness" night. Families could come learn basic skills, and there could be a reading corner for kids who wanted to take breaks. Hot chocolate for everyone, maybe some book recommendations about courage and self-advocacy.

The more he thought about it, the more the idea took shape. Mrs. Zhang would probably help with the hot chocolate—she was always looking for ways to support community events. And if they had a reading component, maybe they could invite the school librarian to help with book selections.

Maybe they could invite Naomi.

He took a sip of his tea and let himself imagine it: Naomi in his space, comfortable and laughing, helping kids find books while Omari practiced his break-falls nearby. The picture was so clear it made his chest ache with wanting.

Don't compete off the mat, he reminded himself. But was it competing to want to create a space where she felt safe? Was it competing to hope that maybe, if he was patient and careful and proved himself worthy of her trust, she might see him as more than just her son's martial arts instructor?

His phone buzzed. A text from his sister in Atlanta:

> How's the dojo? Still teaching people how to fall down on purpose?

He smiled despite himself; he typed back,

Teaching them how to get back up on purpose

Same thing, different angle. You happy?

The question stopped him. Was he happy? The dojo was successful, he had good students, he was doing work that mattered. He had a comfortable life, good friends, a place in the community.

But sitting here thinking about Naomi Ellis, about the worry lines around her eyes and the way she'd looked at him like he might actually have answers to her problems—he realized happiness wasn't the same as contentment. And contentment wasn't the same as fulfillment.

Getting there, one day at a time.

Good. Mom says to tell you she's proud of you.

Tell her I said thanks.

He finished his tea and walked the few blocks home to his small house on Maple Street. The place was neat and quiet, exactly as he'd left it. Books on the shelf, dishes washed and put away, everything in its place.

But tonight the orderliness felt less peaceful and more empty. He found himself wondering what it would be like to come home to the sound of voices, to homework spread across the kitchen table, to the comfortable chaos of a family.

Before bed, he pulled out the journal he'd been keeping since opening the dojo. It was a habit left over from his military days —writing down thoughts and observations, tracking patterns, noting lessons learned.

He wrote:

New students today.

Omari Ellis, 10, dealing with bullying at school. Natural ability, good instincts. Mother is Naomi Ellis— we went to high school together. She's cautious but willing to try. Both need confidence more than technique right now.

HE PAUSED, pen hovering over the paper. Then he added:

Reminder to self—don't rush what deserves time. Some things are worth the patience.

He closed the journal and turned off the light, but sleep was a long time coming. Instead, he lay in the dark thinking about second chances and the difference between wanting to help someone and wanting to keep them. About the way Naomi's hand had trembled when she'd held that flyer, and how Omari's whole face had lit up when he'd successfully completed his first break-fall.

Tomorrow they'd be back. Tomorrow he'd have another chance to show them that his dojo was a safe place, that he was someone they could trust.

Tomorrow he'd try to remember that the best way to care for someone was to give them exactly what they needed, nothing more and nothing less.

Even if what they needed wasn't him.

The lunch tray incident happened at exactly 11:47 AM. Naomi knew the precise time because she'd been checking the clock every few minutes since lunch period started, her stomach twisted in knots despite being tucked safely away in the children's library. Mrs. Rivera found her twenty minutes later, looking grim.

"We need to talk," the counselor said, closing the library door behind her. "Parent hat, not staff hat."

Naomi's hands stilled on the picture books she'd been shelving. "What happened?"

"Marcus Henderson 'accidentally' bumped into Omari at the tray line. Knocked his lunch to the floor. When Omari bent to clean it up, Marcus said something that made three other kids laugh."

The familiar burn of helpless anger flared in Naomi's chest. "What did he say?"

"Something about how his mom works at the school but can't even protect him. How maybe they should both just leave town since nobody wants them here anyway."

The books in Naomi's hands suddenly felt impossibly heavy. She set them down carefully, afraid she might drop them.

"Where's Omari now?"

"Eating lunch in my office. He asked if he could call you, but I thought I'd check first." Mrs. Rivera's voice was gentle but firm. "Naomi, I know this is hard to hear as his mother. But as his counselor, I need to tell you—he handled it exactly right. He didn't engage, didn't escalate. He just cleaned up his lunch and walked away. Then he came straight to find me."

He handled it exactly right. The words should have been comforting, but instead they made Naomi want to scream. Her ten-year-old son was becoming an expert at de-escalating bullies, and somehow that was supposed to be a victory.

"I want to see him," she said.

"Of course. But Naomi?" Mrs. Rivera touched her arm gently. "When you do, remember you're his safe place. He needs to see that you believe he's strong enough to handle this, because he is. He's stronger than he knows."

The counselor left, and Naomi stood alone among the bright picture books and cheerful reading posters, feeling like the world's biggest fraud. How was she supposed to convince her son he was strong enough to handle bullies when she couldn't even handle her ex-husband's text messages without her hands shaking?

Her phone buzzed as if summoned by her thoughts. Andre again:

> Omari called me upset about something at school. We need to discuss better communication. I shouldn't have to hear about my son's problems secondhand.

She stared at the message, trying to decode the manipulation. Omari hadn't called his father—Andre must have heard something through the small-town gossip network. But by framing it as if Omari had reached out to him, Andre was setting up his next attack: that she was keeping him out of the loop, being a bad co-parent, probably planning to argue that she was an unfit mother.

She took a screenshot for her documentation folder and typed back carefully:

> School incidents are handled through proper channels. All information will be shared through the parent portal as required by our custody agreement.

His response came immediately:

> Don't hide behind bureaucracy when our son needs his father.

She didn't answer. Instead, she walked to Mrs. Rivera's office to collect Omari for the rest of their lunch period.

At 3:55, Naomi stood outside Sweetgum Jiu-Jitsu & Wellness with two sets of workout clothes in a borrowed gym bag, trying to convince herself this wasn't a mistake. Beside her, Omari bounced on his toes, all nervous energy and barely contained excitement.

"What if I'm terrible at it?" he asked for the third time.

"What if you're wonderful at it?" she countered, though her own stomach was doing somersaults.

"What if the other kids are better than me?"

"Then you'll learn from them."

"What if—"

"Omari." She crouched down to his level, taking his hands in hers. "What if we just try it and see what happens? What if we trust that Mr. Khadir knows what he's doing?"

He nodded, but she could see the worry still swimming in his eyes. The lunch incident had shaken him more than he was letting on, and she wondered if this was too much too soon. Maybe they should have waited, given him more time to process—

The door opened, and Khadir appeared as if he'd been watching for them.

"Right on time," he said, his voice warm and certain. "Ready to learn something new?"

Something about his presence immediately steadied her nerves. He looked exactly like what he was—someone who knew how to keep people safe, someone who'd thought carefully about how to help them.

"We brought workout clothes," Omari said, holding up his corner of the gym bag.

"Perfect. Changing rooms are right through there. Take your time."

When they emerged in t-shirts and yoga pants, Kiana was waiting with a clipboard and two sets of loaner equipment.

"Mouth guards for later," she explained, "and these are foam rollers for warm-up. Today we're focusing on foundation work —how to move, how to breathe, how to create space."

The dojo felt different in the early evening light. More intimate somehow, with just six other students scattered across the mats. Naomi recognized two of them from school pickup—Mrs. Thompson's daughter Sarah and the Johnsons' boy Michael. Normal kids from normal families, here to learn confidence and self-control.

"Adults over here," Khadir said, gesturing to one corner of the mat. "Kids with Kiana."

Naomi watched Omari bow onto the mat with the other children, his movements careful and deliberate. Already he looked more settled than he had all day.

"How are you feeling?" Khadir asked as she joined him in the adult section.

"Nervous," she admitted. "I've never done anything like this."

"That's normal. We'll start simple." He settled onto the mat, patting the space across from him. "Same position as yesterday—one hand on my collarbone, one at my hip. Your frame, your safe space."

She knelt facing him, placed her hands where he'd shown her. This close, she could see the gold flecks in his brown eyes, could smell the clean scent of his gi. Her heart did something complicated against her ribs.

"Breathe," he said softly. "Wide and steady. There's no rush here."

She tried for a deep breath and felt it catch, then slowly expand. Across the room, she could hear Kiana counting out break-falls, the soft rhythm of small bodies learning to fall safely.

"Good. Now, yesterday we worked on the hip escape—making space by sliding away. Today we're going to add something called a technical stand-up. It's exactly what it sounds like—getting to your feet with intention, not panic."

He demonstrated from the seated position, posting his hand, bringing his outside foot up, rising in one fluid motion that looked like choreography.

"The key is the posting hand," he explained. "It gives you base, stability. You're not scrambling to get up—you're choosing to get up, step by step."

She tried it, feeling clumsy and off-balance. Her hand slipped on the mat, and she had to catch herself from falling backward.

"It's okay," Khadir said. "Everyone's wobbly the first few times. Here—"

He moved closer, his hand covering hers on the mat. "Post

here, like you're pushing the earth away from you. Feel how that gives you stability?"

His hand was warm and steady over hers, and something about the contact made her breathing even out. She tried again, and this time the movement clicked.

"Better," he said, and she could hear the smile in his voice. "Again."

They practiced the sequence—hip escape to make space, technical stand-up to gain her feet, return to ready position. Over and over until her body began to remember the rhythm of it.

"Why this?" she asked during a water break. "Why not just... I don't know, learn to punch things?"

"Because creating distance is almost always better than creating damage," he said. "If you can make space, you have options. If you're trapped in close, you're just reacting to whatever someone else decides to do to you."

The words hit deeper than technique instruction. *If you're trapped in close, you're just reacting.* That's exactly how she'd felt for months—reactive, defensive, always one step behind Andre's next manipulation.

"Makes sense," she said quietly.

"Plus," Khadir added with a slight smile, "learning to fall safely and get up on purpose—those are life skills. They work just as well in a boardroom as they do in a parking lot."

Or in a school cafeteria, Naomi thought. Or dealing with an ex-husband who couldn't accept that the marriage was over.

They returned to drilling, and something began to shift in her body. The movements became smoother, more natural. Her breathing stayed steady even when Khadir increased the pace slightly. For the first time in months, her mind felt quiet—focused on just this moment, just this movement, just the simple task of learning something new.

"Excellent," Khadir said after she completed a sequence without hesitation. "You're getting it."

Across the room, Omari was working on his break-falls with intense concentration, his tongue poking out slightly as he focused. When he nailed a particularly smooth roll, he looked over at her with bright eyes.

"Mom, did you see that?"

"I saw it," she called back. "That looked professional."

He beamed and immediately tried it again.

"He's doing well," Khadir observed. "Kiana says he's got good spatial awareness. Some kids rush the technique, but he's taking his time to understand it first."

"He's always been thoughtful like that. Sometimes I worry he thinks too much."

"Thinking isn't the enemy," Khadir said. "Overthinking is. But what he's doing—that's not overthinking. That's learning."

They worked through the rest of the class, and by the end, Naomi's legs were pleasantly tired and her mind was... quiet. Not empty, but settled in a way she hadn't felt in months.

During the final stretch, she found herself studying Khadir's profile as he demonstrated a breathing exercise. The strong line of his jaw, the way his hands moved with such precise control, the patience in his voice as he corrected someone's form. He'd built something good here—a place where people could learn to be stronger without having to be harder.

"Before we finish," he said, "confidence logs."

He handed out index cards, and Naomi found herself writing without having to think: *Learned to get up on purpose. Felt steady.*

When she handed it back, their fingers brushed briefly, and she caught him reading it. The smile that crossed his face was soft and proud, like he'd been hoping to see exactly those words.

"Same time Thursday?" he asked as they collected their things.

"Yes," Omari said before she could answer. "Definitely yes."

"I guess that's a yes," she said, and found herself smiling.

Walking back to the car, Omari chattered about break-falls and technical stand-ups, his whole body animated in a way that made her heart lift. When they stopped at the red light on Pine Street, her phone buzzed with another message from Andre, but for the first time in weeks, she didn't feel the familiar spike of anxiety.

Instead, she remembered the feeling of posting her hand on the mat, of choosing to stand up step by step, of creating space and distance on her own terms.

If you can make space, you have options.

Maybe it was time to start believing that.

At home, they heated up leftover soup and did homework at the kitchen table, both of them moving with a kind of relaxed tiredness that felt earned. When Omari finished his math worksheet—the same one he'd been struggling with the night before—he looked up at her with something new in his expression.

"Mom? I think I like feeling strong."

"Me too, baby," she said, and meant it. "Me too."

That night, after Omari was asleep, she sat on her back porch with a cup of tea and let herself really feel the events of the day. The lunch incident still stung, and Andre's messages still made her angry. But underneath those familiar emotions was something new—a sense that maybe, possibly, she didn't have to just endure these challenges. Maybe she could learn to meet them differently.

Get up on purpose, she thought, watching the stars appear one by one over Sweetgum. *Step by step.*

For the first time in months, the quiet that followed didn't feel fragile. It felt like a foundation she could build on.

CHAPTER FOUR

*T*hursday's kids' class was running long, but Khadir didn't mind. Tyler had finally mastered his forward roll, and little Sarah Thompson was nailing her break-falls with the kind of precision that made him proud to be her instructor. In the corner, Omari worked through his sequences with quiet focus, taking his time with each movement like he was solving a puzzle.

"Don't rush it," Khadir called to the group. "Perfect practice makes perfect. Sloppy practice just makes you good at being sloppy."

Omari's head popped up. "What if you're already sloppy?"

"Then you start over. Clean slate, try again." Khadir moved to kneel beside him. "Show me your technical stand-up."

The boy moved through the sequence—posting his hand, bringing his foot up, rising with control. It wasn't flawless, but it was solid. More importantly, it was confident.

"That looked like someone who knows what he's doing," Khadir said. "How did it feel?"

"Like I could do it even if someone was watching," Omari said, then seemed surprised by his own words.

"That's exactly right. The technique should feel the same whether you're alone or in front of a hundred people." Khadir glanced at the clock. "Speaking of which, your mom will be here soon. Want to show her that sequence?"

Omari's face lit up. "You think she'll be impressed?"

"I think she'll be proud. But more importantly, you should be proud."

The other kids began filtering out with their parents, and Khadir found himself checking the door more frequently than usual. At exactly four o'clock, Naomi appeared, still in her work clothes but carrying the gym bag that meant she was committed to this.

"How was the day?" he asked as she signed Omari in for the adult class.

"Better," she said, and he caught something different in her voice. Steadier. "Omari wants to show you something."

"Mom, watch this." Omari demonstrated his technical stand-up sequence, and Naomi's face transformed as she watched. Pride, relief, and something that looked suspiciously like hope all mixed together in her expression.

"That was beautiful," she said, and Khadir could tell she meant it. "You looked so... intentional."

"That's the word," Khadir said. "Intentional movement instead of reactive movement."

The adult class was smaller tonight—just Naomi, Mr. Peterson from the hardware store, and Mrs. Rodriguez, whose daughter was in Omari's grade. Kiana took the kids to the other side of the mat for their own session.

"Tonight we're going to work on something a little different," Khadir said once they'd warmed up. "It's called a scissor sweep. Don't worry—no one's throwing anyone. It's more like a gentle tip-and-roll."

He demonstrated slowly, showing how to hook one leg and use leverage rather than strength to off-balance a partner. "The beautiful thing about this technique is it doesn't matter how big or strong your opponent is. Physics does the work."

Mr. Peterson, who was at least sixty and had been dealing with teenagers shoplifting in his store, perked up with interest. "Show me that again."

Khadir worked with him while Naomi partnered with Mrs. Rodriguez. But he found his attention constantly drifting to Naomi's side of the mat, noting how she moved, how she processed instructions, how her confidence had grown since that first nervous day.

"Switch partners," he called after fifteen minutes. "Mrs. Rodriguez, work with Mr. Peterson. Naomi, you're with me."

She settled across from him on the mat, and he tried to ignore the way his pulse quickened when she placed her hands in position. Professional, he reminded himself. This was about teaching, not about the way her hair had escaped its ponytail or how her cheeks were flushed from exertion.

"Ready to try the scissor sweep?" he asked.

"I think so. Though I'm not sure I understand the physics part."

"Here, let me show you." He guided her through the movement at quarter speed, his hands covering hers to demonstrate the angle. "It's not about pulling or pushing. It's about creating the right angle and letting momentum do the work."

She tried it, tentative at first. The sweep was gentle but effective, and Khadir allowed himself to roll with it, coming to rest on his back on the mat.

"Oh!" Naomi looked startled by her own success. "Did I do that right?"

"Perfectly." He rolled back up to sitting, grinning. "Want to try it at half speed?"

They worked through the technique several more times, and with each repetition, Naomi grew more confident. By the end of the drilling session, she was executing the sweep with smooth precision.

"That felt..." She paused, searching for words. "Powerful. But not aggressive."

"That's the difference between force and technique," he said. "Force is about overwhelming someone. Technique is about understanding leverage and timing."

They were interrupted by two parents appearing in the doorway—a couple Khadir didn't recognize, both wearing expensive workout gear and skeptical expressions.

"Excuse me," the woman called. "Is this some kind of mixed martial arts place? We heard there might be hitting?"

Khadir rose smoothly, noting how Naomi tensed slightly at the interruption. "No hitting in our programs," he said calmly. "We focus on defensive techniques—how to create space, how to move safely, how to avoid confrontation when possible."

"But what if someone attacks you?" the man asked. "Don't you need to know how to fight back?"

"The best fight is the one you don't have to have," Khadir replied. "Most dangerous situations can be avoided with good awareness and basic defensive skills. We teach people how to get away safely, not how to hurt others."

The couple exchanged glances. "What about for kids? Don't they need to learn to stand up to bullies?"

Out of the corner of his eye, Khadir saw Omari's head turn toward the conversation. The boy had been working on his break-falls, but now he was listening intently.

"They do need to learn to stand up for themselves," Khadir said carefully. "But standing up doesn't always mean fighting. Sometimes it means having the confidence to walk away. Sometimes it means knowing how to get help. And sometimes it means having the skills to create distance if someone won't leave you alone."

"Sounds like running away to me," the man muttered.

"There's a difference between running away in fear and choosing not to engage from a position of strength," Khadir said, his voice remaining patient. "We teach the latter."

The couple left without signing up, and Khadir returned to the group. But he noticed Naomi watching him with something new in her expression—appreciation, maybe, or respect.

"That was well handled," she said quietly.

"Not everyone understands what we do here. That's okay." He glanced over at Omari, who had returned to his drilling but was still listening. "The right people find their way to us."

They finished class with stretching and confidence logs. Omari wrote

Did the sweep like Mr. Khadir

in his careful handwriting. Naomi's card said

Felt powerful without being mean.

As they packed up their things, Khadir's phone chimed with a direct message notification. He glanced at it briefly—an anonymous account asking questions about his "dating policies" with clients—then quickly put the phone away.

"Everything okay?" Naomi asked.

"Just someone with questions about the dojo," he said. It wasn't exactly a lie. "Kiana handles most of our social media, but sometimes people message me directly."

He made a mental note to show Kiana the message later. They'd had to deal with inappropriate inquiries before—usually from people who'd seen too many movies and thought martial arts instructors were either dangerous or romantic interests rather than teachers.

"Before you go," he said, pulling a flyer from behind the front desk. "I'm organizing a community event for next month. 'Confidence and Kindness Night.' Families can come try some basic techniques, and we're setting up a reading corner for kids who want to take breaks. I was hoping..." He paused, suddenly uncertain. "Well, since you work at the school library, I thought you might have ideas for book recommendations. About courage, or standing up for yourself, that kind of thing."

Naomi's face brightened. "I'd love to help with that. There are some wonderful books about inner strength and self-advocacy that would be perfect."

"Great. Would you mind if I stopped by the school sometime to discuss it? Or we could meet at Roasted Beans if that's easier."

"The school would be fine," she said. "I'm usually there until four most days, setting up for the next day or working on displays."

"Perfect. I'll call ahead so you know I'm coming."

As they walked toward the door, Omari tugged on Khadir's gi. "Mr. Khadir? What you said to those people about standing up without fighting—is that what I'm supposed to do with Marcus and Devin?"

Khadir knelt down to the boy's level. "What do you think? You've been learning these techniques for a few days now. How do you feel when you practice them?"

"Stronger," Omari said immediately. "Like I don't have to be scared."

"And when you're not scared, how do you think you walk? How do you think you hold your shoulders?"

Omari straightened up unconsciously, demonstrating Khadir's point.

"Bullies look for easy targets," Khadir said gently. "They want people who seem scared or uncertain. When you walk like someone who knows how to take care of himself, when you move with intention instead of fear—that changes how people see you."

"But what if they still bother me?"

"Then you use your voice first. Clear, confident, loud enough for adults to hear. 'Stop. Leave me alone.' And if they don't stop, you make distance and get help."

"And if I can't make distance?"

Khadir met Naomi's eyes over Omari's head. This was the question every parent worried about, the scenario that kept them awake at night.

"Then you use what we've taught you to create space and get away. Not to hurt anyone, but to protect yourself and get to safety." His voice was firm but gentle. "But Omari? The goal is never to fight. The goal is always to get safe."

The boy nodded solemnly. "I understand."

"Good man."

As they walked to their car, Khadir heard Omari chattering to his mother about the scissor sweep and how "physics does the work." Naomi's responses were engaged and encouraging, but Khadir caught her looking back at the dojo with an expression he couldn't quite read.

Thoughtful, maybe. Or grateful.

Or maybe something more complicated than either.

Back inside, Kiana was wiping down mats and humming under her breath.

"So," she said without looking up, "how long are you going to pretend this is just about teaching martial arts?"

"What's that supposed to mean?"

"The way you looked at her during that sweep drill. The way you lit up when she said she'd help with the reading corner. The way you found excuses to visit her at work." Kiana grinned. "Should I go ahead and plan your wedding or what?"

"It's not like that," Khadir said automatically.

"Uh-huh. Sure it's not." She straightened, studying his face. "Though I have to say, if it was like that, you could do a lot worse than Naomi Ellis. She's good people, and that boy of hers is something special."

Khadir didn't deny it. How could he? Naomi was good people. And Omari was something special. And if he was being honest with himself, the feelings he'd carried for seventeen years hadn't diminished—they'd just gotten deeper and more complicated.

"It's about helping them," he said finally.

"Can't it be both?"

The question hung in the air between them, and Khadir didn't have a good answer. Maybe because the honest answer was too dangerous to say out loud.

Maybe because the honest answer was yes, it could be both, and that terrified him more than any opponent he'd ever faced on a mat.

CHAPTER FIVE

$\mathcal{N}$aomi stood in front of her closet at 6:30 PM, holding two different cardigans and trying to convince herself this wasn't a date.

Mia was reading at Roasted Beans Coffee Spot's monthly open mic night. As her best friend and fellow teacher, Mia had specifically asked Naomi to come support her. The fact that Khadir had mentioned yesterday that he planned to stop by to post his Confidence & Kindness Night flyer was purely coincidental.

The fact that she'd changed clothes twice was also purely coincidental.

"Mom, you look nervous," Omari observed from her bedroom doorway. He was in his pajamas, ready for his sleepover at Mia's house with her nephew Tyler. "Are you going on a date?"

"I'm going to support Mia," she said firmly, settling on the navy cardigan. "Friends support friends."

"But you're wearing the pretty earrings."

She caught her reflection in the mirror. She was indeed

wearing the pretty earrings—the silver ones her grandmother had given her for graduation. When had she put those on?

"I always wear nice earrings," she lied.

"No, you don't. You wear the boring studs except for church and when you like someone."

Out of the mouths of babes. Her ten-year-old son had just called her out with devastating accuracy.

"Get your overnight bag," she said, deflecting. "Mia's expecting us in fifteen minutes."

"Are you going to hold hands with Mr. Khadir?"

"Omari."

"Are you going to kiss him?"

"Omari Ellis, get your bag right now."

He scampered off, giggling, leaving Naomi to stare at herself in the mirror. Was this a date? Could it be a date if only one person knew it was happening?

Her phone buzzed: a text from Andre.

> Omari staying somewhere tonight? We should discuss his weekend schedule.

She took a screenshot and typed back:

> Weekend schedule follows custody agreement as always. See you Sunday at 6 PM for pickup.

His response was immediate:

> Don't be difficult, Naomi. I'm trying to be flexible here.

She didn't respond. Andre's version of "flexible" usually meant changing plans to suit his convenience while framing it as consideration for Omari. She'd fallen for that manipulation too many times during their marriage.

~

Roasted Beans was packed by the time they arrived. The usual tables had been pushed aside to make room for folding chairs arranged in loose rows, and a small stage area was set up near the windows. The warm smell of coffee and cinnamon rolls mixed with the sound of nervous laughter and rustling papers as performers prepared.

"Aunt Naomi!" Tyler bounced over to collect Omari, and the boys immediately began planning their evening of video games and junk food. Mia appeared behind them, clutching a notebook and looking slightly green.

"I can't believe I signed up for this," she said, hugging Naomi. "What was I thinking? I teach second grade. I don't perform poetry in front of adults."

"You teach second grade," Naomi corrected. "Which means you perform in front of the toughest audience in the world every single day. Adults are easy."

"Adults don't ask if you need to use the bathroom in the middle of your presentation."

"No, but they're much more forgiving about forgotten lines."

Mia took a shaky breath. "You're right. I can do this. I read to children professionally. This is just... reading to bigger children."

"Exactly." Naomi squeezed her friend's hand. "I'll be right here cheering you on."

They found seats in the third row, close enough for moral support but not so close that Mia would be distracted by Naomi's encouraging nods. The first few performers took the stage—a high school student reading original slam poetry, Mrs. Henderson from the school office singing an old hymn, Mr. Chen from the watch repair shop playing acoustic guitar.

Naomi was genuinely enjoying the evening, caught up in the community spirit and her friend's nervous energy, when she heard a familiar voice behind her.

"Is this seat taken?"

She turned to find Khadir holding a cup of tea and a folded

flyer, looking uncertain. He was wearing dark jeans and a green button-down that made his eyes look warm gold in the coffee shop's lighting.

"It's open," she said, trying to ignore the way her pulse quickened. "Did you get your flyer posted?"

"Joanne said I could put it up during the break." He settled into the chair beside her, close enough that she could smell his cologne—something clean and woodsy that made her want to lean closer. "How's Mia feeling?"

"Terrified. She's reading a piece about teaching that she wrote for the school newsletter, but performing it feels different than just submitting it for publication."

"I remember her from high school," Khadir said quietly. "She was always braver than she thought."

The current performer finished to warm applause, and Joanne took the microphone to introduce the next reader. "Please welcome Mia Patterson, reading an original piece called 'What They Don't Tell You About Teaching.'"

Mia walked to the microphone on slightly unsteady legs, adjusted the height, and looked out at the audience. Her eyes found Naomi's, and Naomi gave her the most encouraging smile she could manage.

"This is about why I became a teacher," Mia began, her voice gaining strength as she spoke. "And what I've learned about the difference between teaching subjects and teaching people."

What followed was beautiful—a thoughtful, funny, heartfelt meditation on the unexpected moments that made teaching worthwhile. The time a struggling reader finally conquered a difficult book. The way children's faces lit up when they grasped a new concept. The privilege of being trusted with young minds and hearts during their most formative years.

"Teaching isn't just about curriculum," Mia concluded. "It's about seeing potential in people who don't yet see it in themselves. It's about believing in someone until they learn to believe in themselves."

The applause was genuine and sustained. Mia practically glowed as she returned to her seat, and Naomi felt tears prick her eyes.

"That was incredible," she whispered as Mia sat down.

"I can't believe I did that," Mia whispered back. "I actually did that."

"You were amazing," Khadir leaned over to say. "That piece about believing in people until they believe in themselves—that's exactly what good teaching is."

Mia beamed. "Thank you. Though I have to say, from what I hear, you do the same thing at your dojo."

"I try."

During the break, Khadir excused himself to post his flyer while Naomi and Mia got refills on their drinks. Several people approached Mia to compliment her reading, and Naomi watched her friend bask in the well-deserved praise.

"So," Mia said when they had a moment alone, "Khadir Grant looks good."

"Mia."

"I'm just saying. He's gotten even more handsome since high school, if that's possible. And the way he was looking at you during my reading..." She waggled her eyebrows. "Very attentive."

"He was listening to you read."

"Honey, no. He was listening to you breathe. There's a difference."

Heat climbed Naomi's neck. "You're imagining things."

"Am I? Because he's been checking to make sure you're okay every five minutes since he sat down. And when you laughed at that funny line in my piece, he got this little smile like he was proud of you for enjoying yourself."

Before Naomi could protest, Khadir returned with his tea and a small plate of cookies.

"Joanne said these were fresh," he said, offering the plate to both women. "Thought you might want to try them."

"Thank you," Naomi said, acutely aware of Mia watching the interaction with barely concealed amusement. "That was thoughtful."

The second half of the open mic featured a wider variety of performers—more music, some storytelling, a group of teenagers doing spoken word about social media. Naomi found herself relaxing into the evening, enjoying the community atmosphere and the creative energy in the room.

When the official program ended around nine, people lingered to chat and congratulate performers. Mia was surrounded by a small crowd of admirers, and the boys were deep in conversation with some other kids about a video game tournament.

"Would you like to walk?" Khadir asked quietly. "It's a nice evening, and it might be a while before Mia's ready to leave."

Naomi looked around the crowded coffee shop, then at Khadir's patient expression. "A short walk would be nice."

They stepped outside into the soft September air. Pine Street was quiet except for the warm light spilling from shop windows and the distant sound of the open mic continuing inside Roasted Beans.

"That was fun," Naomi said as they began walking slowly toward the town square. "I don't get out to community events as much as I should."

"Why not?"

The question was gentle, but it made her think. Why didn't she get out more? Because she was tired after work and parenting alone? Because Andre had made socializing feel complicated during their marriage? Because it was easier to stay home than to navigate the questions and well-meaning advice that came with being a divorced single mother in a small town?

"I guess I got out of the habit," she said finally.

"It's good to see you enjoying yourself. You looked relaxed tonight."

"I felt relaxed. It's been a while since I've done something just for fun."

They walked in comfortable silence for a few minutes, their footsteps echoing softly on the sidewalk. When they reached the town square, Khadir gestured to one of the benches facing the gazebo.

"Want to sit for a minute?"

She nodded, settling onto the bench with a careful distance between them. The night air was soft and sweet, carrying the scent of the late-blooming flowers in the square's garden beds.

"Thank you," she said.

"For what?"

"For making tonight feel... normal. Easy." She turned to look at him. "It's been a long time since something felt easy."

His expression grew serious. "Divorce is hard. Especially when there are kids involved."

"It's not just the divorce," she found herself saying. "It's the aftermath. Andre doesn't like boundaries, and he's very good at making me feel like I'm being unreasonable for having them."

Khadir was quiet for a moment, and she wondered if she'd said too much. They were building a friendship, maybe something more, but her baggage with Andre wasn't his problem.

"Boundaries aren't unreasonable," he said finally. "They're necessary. And anyone who tries to make you feel bad for having them..." He shook his head. "That says something about them, not about you."

The simple validation hit deeper than she'd expected. Andre had spent their entire marriage convincing her that her need for space, respect, and consideration was somehow selfish. Hearing

Khadir say the opposite—firmly, without hesitation—felt like being given permission to trust her own instincts.

"The jiu-jitsu helps," she said. "Learning to create space, learning to move with intention instead of just reacting. It's good for more than just physical situations."

"That's the idea. Confidence is confidence, whether you're dealing with someone grabbing your arm or someone trying to manipulate your emotions."

They sat in comfortable silence, watching the stars appear one by one above the gazebo. Somewhere in the distance, a dog barked once and then settled. The night felt peaceful in a way Naomi hadn't experienced in months.

"I should get back," she said eventually. "Mia's probably wondering where I went."

"Of course." Khadir stood and offered her his hand to help her up from the bench.

She took it without thinking, and the simple contact sent warmth up her arm. His hand was callused from martial arts training but gentle, steady. When she was on her feet, he didn't immediately let go.

"Naomi," he said quietly.

"Yes?"

"I'm glad you came tonight. And I'm glad we got to walk."

"Me too."

They were standing close now, her hand still in his, and she could see the flecks of gold in his brown eyes. For a moment, the air between them felt charged with possibility.

Then her phone buzzed with a text notification, and the spell broke. She reluctantly pulled her hand free to check the message.

Andre again:

> Need to discuss Omari's school situation. This can't wait until Sunday.

The familiar knot of anxiety formed in her stomach, but this time it was accompanied by something else. Irritation. She was having a lovely evening—her first genuinely relaxing night in months—and Andre was trying to pull her back into his drama.

"Everything okay?" Khadir asked, noting her expression.

"Just my ex-husband trying to manufacture an emergency that requires immediate attention." She put the phone away without responding. "It can wait until our scheduled communication time."

"Good for you."

The approval in his voice warmed her more than it should have. They walked back toward Roasted Beans, and as they approached the coffee shop's glowing windows, Khadir slowed.

"Would it be okay if I asked you to have dinner sometime? Just the two of us?"

Her heart did something complicated against her ribs. "Are you asking me on a date, Khadir Grant?"

A slow smile spread across his face. "I'm asking if you'd like to have dinner with me. You can call it whatever feels comfortable."

She thought about Andre's text, about the way he tried to control her time and attention even from a distance. She thought about Mia's reading, about believing in people until they learned to believe in themselves. She thought about the feeling of Khadir's steady hand in hers.

"I'd like that," she said. "I'd like that very much."

"How about Saturday? There's a new Thai place in Peachtree, or we could stay local if you prefer."

"Let's stay local. Maybe Sweet and Spicy Chinese Palace? I haven't been there in ages."

"It's a date," he said, then caught himself. "I mean—"

"It's a date," she agreed, smiling. "A real one this time."

Inside Roasted Beans, Mia was collecting congratulations and the boys were winding down from their sugar rush. As

Naomi gathered her purse and said her goodbyes, she caught Mia watching her with knowing eyes.

"You look happy," Mia observed quietly. "Really happy."

"I feel happy," Naomi admitted. "Terrified, but happy."

"Good terrified or bad terrified?"

Naomi glanced over at Khadir, who was helping Joanne stack chairs and chatting easily with other community members. Solid, dependable, kind. Everything Andre wasn't.

"Good terrified," she said. "Definitely good terrified."

Walking to her car later, Omari already buckled into the backseat and chattering about his evening with Tyler, Naomi let herself feel the full weight of what had just happened. She had a date. A real date with a man who saw her as more than just a difficult ex-wife or a stressed single mother.

Her phone buzzed again—Andre, no doubt, escalating his manufactured emergency. But for once, she didn't feel the familiar spike of anxiety. Instead, she felt something she'd almost forgotten: anticipation for something good.

CHAPTER SIX

$\mathcal{K}$hadir arrived at Sweet and Spicy Chinese Palace ten minutes early, which gave him just enough time to second-guess everything about this evening. Should he have chosen somewhere fancier? Should he have offered to pick Naomi up instead of meeting her here? Should he have worn the blue shirt instead of the gray one?

Mrs. Zhang spotted him hovering near the entrance and waved him over to the counter with a knowing smile.

"You look nervous," she observed, wiping her hands on her apron. "This wouldn't have anything to do with a certain school librarian, would it?"

Heat climbed up Khadir's neck. "How did you—"

"Honey, this is Sweetgum. I heard about your dinner plans before you probably finished asking her." Mrs. Zhang's expression softened. "Naomi's good people. That boy of hers too. They deserve someone who treats them right."

"I'm hoping to do exactly that."

"I know you are. Which is why I'm putting you at table seven —the one by the window with the good light, but not so visible that half the town will be watching you eat." She grabbed two menus and a small thermos from behind the counter. "And I'm sending you home with hot chocolate mix for the boy. Homemade, not the powder stuff."

"Mrs. Zhang, you don't have to—"

"Course I don't have to. I want to." She patted his arm maternally. "Some things are worth celebrating, even before they're fully grown."

The bell above the door chimed, and Khadir turned to see Naomi stepping inside. She wore a deep blue dress that complemented her warm skin tone and made his breath catch slightly. She'd left her natural curls loose, the full texture framing her face beautifully, and when she spotted him, her smile was genuine and maybe a little nervous.

"Right on time," he said, moving to greet her.

"I'm usually early, but I spent twenty minutes trying to find my car keys." She held up her purse with a rueful smile. "Omari finally found them in the refrigerator."

"The refrigerator?"

"I was putting away groceries while checking my work email. Apparently multitasking has its limits."

Mrs. Zhang appeared beside them with menus. "Table seven is ready for you. Take your time, no rush."

They settled into the corner booth, and Khadir tried to ignore how intimate the space felt with the late afternoon light slanting through the windows. Naomi looked around the restaurant appreciatively.

"I haven't been here since before my divorce," she said. "Andre always wanted to go to chain restaurants when we ate out. Said local places were 'unpredictable.'"

"What did he mean by that?"

"The food might be different from what he expected. The service might be slower than a drive-through. People might actually talk to us." She shook her head. "He liked everything controlled and predictable."

Khadir filed that information away with everything else he was learning about Naomi's marriage. Andre sounded like the kind of man who saw other people as variables to be managed rather than individuals to be respected.

"Well, Mrs. Zhang's cooking is definitely predictable," he said. "Predictably excellent."

Naomi laughed. "That's the kind of predictable I can handle."

They ordered—sweet and sour chicken for her, beef and broccoli for him, spring rolls to share. As they waited for their food, the conversation flowed easier than Khadir had expected. They talked about the dojo's Confidence and Kindness Night, about books Naomi recommended for the reading corner, about Omari's progress in martial arts.

"He practiced his break-falls in the backyard yesterday," Naomi said, her face lighting up with pride. "I was doing laundry, and I looked out the window to see him rolling around on the grass, completely focused. When he came inside, he said he was 'training his body to remember.'"

"That's exactly right. Muscle memory is real—the body learns patterns and keeps them."

"Is that how you learned? Just repetition until it became automatic?"

Khadir nodded. "That, and having good teachers who were patient with my mistakes. The military taught me discipline, but martial arts taught me precision. How to be strong without being aggressive, how to be confident without being arrogant."

"Is that why you opened the dojo? To teach those lessons?"

The question made him pause. He could give her the standard answer he gave everyone else—about wanting to serve his community, about believing in practical self-defense skills. But sitting here with Naomi, in the gentle light of Mrs. Zhang's restaurant, he found himself wanting to tell the truth.

"Partly that," he said. "But also because I needed to learn

those lessons myself. The discipline part came easy. The confidence without arrogance part... that took longer."

"What do you mean?"

"I spent a lot of years thinking I had to prove myself worthy of things. Worthy of respect, worthy of success, worthy of..." He caught himself before he said 'worthy of you.' "Worthy of good things, I guess. The dojo taught me that worthiness isn't something you earn through perfect performance. It's something you already have."

Naomi's expression grew thoughtful. "That's a hard lesson. I'm still learning it myself."

"Your ex-husband made you feel like you had to earn basic respect?"

The question came out sharper than he'd intended, but Naomi didn't seem offended. Instead, she considered it carefully.

"He made me feel like love was conditional. Like if I could just be the right kind of wife, do the right things, say the right words, then he'd treat me the way I wanted to be treated. It took me years to realize that wasn't love—that was management."

The word landed heavy between them. Management. Like she'd been a project to be optimized rather than a person to be cherished.

"I'm sorry," he said quietly. "No one should have to live like that."

"I'm learning to live differently now. The jiu-jitsu helps—all that practice creating space, moving with intention instead of just reacting. It's good training for more than just physical situations."

Their food arrived, and they spent the next hour talking about everything and nothing. Naomi told him about the kids at school, about the reading programs she was developing, about Omari's latest obsession with lightning facts. Khadir shared stories about his students, about the community events he was planning, about his hopes for expanding the dojo's youth programs.

As the evening wound down, Mrs. Zhang appeared with the thermos of hot chocolate mix and a knowing smile.

"For the boy," she said, pressing it into Khadir's hands. "And for you two—" She set down a plate of fortune cookies. "On the house."

Naomi cracked hers open first, reading the slip of paper with a small smile. "What does yours say?" she asked.

Khadir opened his cookie and read: "Good things come to those who are patient."

"Mine says 'Trust your instincts—they're trying to tell you something important.'" Naomi looked up at him with something soft and hopeful in her expression. "Think the universe is trying to tell us something?"

"Maybe. Or maybe Mrs. Zhang writes her own fortunes."

They both laughed, and Khadir felt something settle in his chest. This was right. This easy conversation, this gentle teasing, this sense of possibility. Whatever was growing between them felt natural and unhurried, like something that had been waiting patiently to unfold.

"Would you like to walk?" he asked as they collected their things. "It's a nice evening, and I'm not quite ready for this to end."

"I'd like that."

They stepped out into the soft September air, and Khadir offered her his arm without thinking. She took it, her hand warm against his sleeve, and they began walking slowly down Pine Street toward the town square.

"Thank you," Naomi said as they passed Justin Time's watch repair shop. "This was lovely. I'd forgotten how nice it is to have dinner with someone who actually wants to hear what you have to say."

"I want to hear everything you have to say," Khadir said, then worried that sounded too intense. "I mean—"

"I know what you mean." Her hand tightened slightly on his arm. "It's been a long time since I felt like someone was genuinely interested in my thoughts instead of just waiting for their turn to talk."

They reached the town square, where the evening light was fading to purple and the first stars were appearing. Without discussing it, they gravitated toward the same bench they'd sat on after the open mic night.

"Can I ask you something?" Naomi said once they'd settled.

"Of course."

"Why didn't you ever get married? I always thought... I mean, in high school, you seemed like the kind of person who'd want a family."

The question hit closer to home than she probably realized. How could he tell her that he'd never found anyone who made him feel the way she had at seventeen? That he'd spent his twenties and early thirties comparing every woman he met to a memory of the girl who'd debated their history teacher with such passion that the whole class leaned forward to listen?

"I guess I never found the right person," he said finally. "Or maybe I found her, but the timing wasn't right."

Something flickered in Naomi's expression—surprise, maybe, or understanding. They sat in comfortable silence for a moment, watching the stars appear one by one above the gazebo.

"The timing's different now," she said quietly.

"Yes, it is."

He turned to look at her, this woman he'd carried in his heart for seventeen years, now sitting beside him in the gathering darkness. Her profile was soft in the starlight, and when she looked back at him, he saw the same careful hope he felt building in his chest.

"Naomi," he said softly.

"Yes?"

"I'd like to kiss you. Would that be okay?"

Her answer was barely a whisper: "Yes."

He leaned closer, giving her time to change her mind, time to pull away if she wanted to. But she didn't pull away. Instead, she met him halfway, her eyes fluttering closed as his lips touched hers.

The kiss was gentle, tentative at first, then deeper as she responded. Her hand came up to rest against his chest, and he could feel her heartbeat through her palm, quick and light like a bird's wings. When they finally broke apart, they stayed close, foreheads almost touching.

"Oh," she breathed.

"Good oh or bad oh?"

"Very good oh." She smiled, and in the starlight, she looked young and hopeful and beautiful. "Very, very good oh."

They sat together for a while longer, her hand in his, talking quietly about small things—the upcoming school year, the dojo's fall schedule, Omari's growing confidence. Normal things that felt extraordinary simply because they were sharing them.

When they finally walked back to their cars, Khadir felt like something fundamental had shifted between them. The careful distance of teacher and student parent had dissolved into something warmer, more personal. When they reached Naomi's car, he opened the door for her, then handed her the thermos of hot chocolate.

"For Omari," he said. "Mrs. Zhang insisted."

"He'll be thrilled. He's been asking for hot chocolate weather."

"Maybe we can make some together sometime. The three of us, I mean." The words came out before he could stop them, and he worried he was moving too fast. "If that would be okay."

"I think that would be very okay," Naomi said, her smile warm and genuine. "I think Omari would like that very much."

As she drove away, Khadir stood in the parking lot watching her taillights disappear around the corner. The evening had gone better than he'd dared to hope. Not just the kiss, though that had been... extraordinary. But the easy conversation, the sense of rightness, the way she'd looked at him like he was someone worth knowing.

His phone buzzed with a text:

Thank you for tonight. Sweet dreams. - N

He typed back:

Thank you for saying yes. See you Thursday for class.

Looking forward to it.

Walking to his own car, Khadir felt lighter than he had in years. The patient waiting, the careful friendship-building, the gradual earning of her trust—it was all leading somewhere good. Something real and lasting and worth every moment he'd spent hoping for a second chance.

Good things really did come to those who were patient.

The dismissal bell rang at 3:10, and Naomi Ellis, school librarian, officially clocked out. She hung her staff badge on its designated hook, gathered her purse, and walked to the parking lot like any other parent picking up their child.

But unlike other parents, she didn't have to wonder where Omari was or how his day had gone. She'd seen him twice during school hours—once when his class came for library time, and once when she'd passed his classroom during her lunch break. Both times, he'd given her a small wave, and she'd responded with the same professional nod she gave every student.

The boundaries were clear, and she was grateful for them. At school, she was Ms. Ellis. At home, she was Mom. And at the dojo... well, at the dojo she was beginning to discover she might be something else entirely.

"Ready for class?" Omari asked as he buckled his seatbelt, already changed into his workout clothes.

"Ready," she said, though her stomach did a small flip at the thought of seeing Khadir. Three days had passed since their dinner date, since that perfect kiss on the town square bench, and she still felt warm every time she thought about it.

They'd texted a few times—nothing dramatic, just small check-ins that felt natural and easy.

> How was your day? Omari mentioned you're reading a new book series to the third-graders. Sleep well.

The kind of messages that suggested he was thinking of her without demanding immediate responses or constant attention.

So different from Andre, who used texts like fishing lines, constantly trying to hook her into emotional conversations or manufactured emergencies.

"Mom, you're smiling at your phone again," Omari observed.

"I'm not smiling at my phone."

"You're smiling and looking at your phone. Same thing."

She put the phone in her purse and started the car. "How was school today? Really?"

"Good. Marcus tried to cut in front of me at lunch, but I just moved to a different spot. No big deal." He said it casually, but she caught the slight straightening of his shoulders. "Mrs. Rivera said I handled it well."

Pride swelled in her chest. A week ago, Marcus cutting in line would have sent Omari into a spiral of anxiety. Now he was problem-solving, creating space, moving through the world with more confidence.

"That sounds like exactly the right choice," she said.

"Mr. Khadir says sometimes the best victory is the one where nobody has to lose."

Mr. Khadir says. Omari had been quoting the dojo instructor with increasing frequency, and each time it made her heart do something complicated. Not jealousy—she was glad her son had found a positive male role model. But something deeper, warmer. Hope, maybe. The possibility that they were both finding something they hadn't known they needed.

THE DOJO FELT different when they walked in, though Naomi couldn't put her finger on exactly how. Same clean mats, same organized equipment, same warm lighting. Maybe the difference was in her, in the way her pulse quickened when she spotted Khadir helping a young student with his uniform tie.

He looked up when he heard the door chime, and their eyes met across the room. His smile was immediate and genuine—not the professional instructor smile, but something warmer. Something that said he was glad to see her specifically, not just another student arriving for class.

"Omari, Naomi." He approached them with his usual steady confidence. "How was everyone's day?"

"Good," Omari said, bouncing slightly on his toes. "I practiced my break-falls in the backyard, and Mom said they looked professional."

"Is that so?" Khadir's eyes crinkled with amusement. "Well, we'll have to see if the backyard training translates to the mat."

As Omari ran off to join the other kids with Kiana, Khadir turned his attention to Naomi. "And how was your day, Ms. Ellis?"

The formal address made her smile. "Are you being funny?"

"Maybe a little. I imagine it's strange, keeping the work role and the mom role separate in the same building."

"You have no idea. This morning I had to bite my tongue when Marcus Henderson's teacher mentioned he'd been having 'boundary issues' with other students. I wanted to say, 'Yes, I'm aware—he's been harassing my son.' But that wasn't a conversation for the library associate to have."

Khadir's expression grew more serious. "That must be frustrating."

"It is. But it's also clarifying. I know exactly what my role is in each situation, and I can act accordingly." She paused, then added, "It's good practice for other areas of life too. Knowing when I'm speaking as a co-parent versus when I'm setting boundaries as an individual person."

She didn't say Andre's name, but from the way Khadir's jaw tightened slightly, she suspected he understood the reference.

"Boundaries are important," he said quietly. "Both the ones we set with other people and the ones we set with ourselves."

There was something in his tone that made her wonder if he was thinking about his own boundaries—the careful line he walked between being her instructor and being... whatever they were becoming.

"Adults over here," Kiana called, and the moment shifted back to class mode.

They worked on review techniques—hip escapes, technical stand-ups, the basics that were becoming second nature. But toward the end of class, Khadir introduced something new.

"Tonight we're adding what we call towel mat," he said, holding up a small hand towel. "It's exactly what it sounds like—we use a towel to practice grip breaks and creating distance."

He demonstrated with one of the other students, showing how to break free from a wrist grab using proper leverage instead of brute force.

"The key is not to pull away—that just creates a tug-of-war," he explained. "Instead, you rotate toward the thumb, where the grip is weakest, and create an opening."

When it was Naomi's turn to practice, Khadir knelt across from her with the towel.

"Grab my wrist," he said. "Like you're trying to stop me from leaving."

She wrapped her fingers around his wrist, noting the warmth of his skin, the steady pulse beneath her palm.

"Now I'm going to break your grip," he said calmly. "Feel how I'm not fighting against your strength—I'm finding the mechanical weakness in your hold."

He rotated his wrist toward her thumb, and her grip simply opened. No force, no struggle, just physics and leverage working together.

"Your turn," he said, offering his wrist.

She tried the technique, clumsy at first, then with growing confidence. Each time she successfully broke his grip, she felt a little surge of satisfaction.

"This is about more than just physical grabs, isn't it?" she asked during a water break.

"What do you mean?"

"The principle. Not fighting against someone else's strength, but finding the weak points in their position and using leverage instead of force."

His smile was proud and knowing. "Exactly. Works in boardrooms, in difficult conversations, in any situation where someone is trying to use their position to control yours."

After class, while the other students filtered out, Omari approached them with bright eyes.

"Mom, watch this," he said. "I want to show you the towel thing."

Khadir handed him a small towel, and Omari demonstrated the grip break with careful precision. When he successfully executed the technique, he looked up at Naomi with such pride that her heart nearly burst.

"That was perfect," she said. "Show me again, but slowly, so I can see exactly what you're doing."

For the next ten minutes, Omari became the instructor, carefully coaching his mother through the technique while Khadir watched with quiet approval. There was something beautiful about it—her son teaching her something he'd learned, both of them growing stronger together.

"I think you've got yourself a assistant instructor," Khadir said as they packed up their things.

"He's a good teacher," Naomi agreed. "Patient and encouraging."

"Wonder where he gets that from."

The compliment sent warmth through her chest, but before she could respond, her phone buzzed with an incoming call. Andre's name flashed on the screen, and her stomach immediately clenched.

"I should take this," she said reluctantly. "It might be about this weekend."

She stepped outside onto the sidewalk and answered on the fourth ring.

"Andre."

"Finally. I've been trying to reach you all day." His voice carried that familiar edge of irritation disguised as concern. "We need to discuss Omari's extracurricular activities."

"What about them?"

"This martial arts thing. I'm hearing things around town, and I'm not comfortable with my son learning violence."

Naomi took a steady breath, drawing on the calm she'd been practicing in class. "Omari is learning self-defense and confidence-building. There's nothing violent about it."

"Right. And I suppose his instructor is completely professional? No personal interest in his students' families?"

The insinuation hit like a slap. In a town the size of Sweetgum, gossip traveled fast, and apparently Andre had heard about her dinner with Khadir.

"Omari's training is about his development and confidence," she said evenly. "Nothing else is your concern."

"Everything about my son is my concern. And I'm concerned that his mother is making decisions based on her personal relationships instead of what's best for him."

"I'm making decisions based on what Omari needs," she said, her voice staying level despite the anger building in her chest. "His confidence has improved dramatically, his anxiety has decreased, and he's learning valuable life skills."

"From a man you're dating."

"From a qualified instructor who cares about his students."

"Naomi, be realistic. This looks bad. A recently divorced woman, taking classes with her son's instructor, having dinner dates around town—"

"Andre." The word came out sharp enough to cut through his manipulation. "My personal life is not your business. Omari's training is beneficial for him, it's been approved by his school counselor, and it will continue. If you have specific concerns about the program itself, you're welcome to observe a class."

"Maybe I will."

"You're welcome to. Just call ahead so the instructor can accommodate visitors."

She ended the call and stood on the sidewalk for a moment, her heart racing but her hands steady. A month ago, that conversation would have left her shaking, second-guessing herself, wondering if Andre was right to question her judgment.

Tonight, she felt clear and certain. She'd used her voice, set boundaries, and refused to be drawn into his emotional manipulation. She'd found the weak points in his argument and used leverage instead of force.

Just like the towel mat.

When she walked back into the dojo, Khadir and Omari were sitting on the bench by the door, having a quiet conversation about something that made her son laugh.

"Everything okay?" Khadir asked, noting her expression.

"Yes," she said, and meant it. "Everything's fine."

On the drive home, Omari chatted about class, about the

new technique, about how he wanted to practice the grip break with his friends at school.

"Mom?" he said as they pulled into their driveway.

"Yes, baby?"

"I like how you looked tonight. During class, I mean. You looked..." He paused, searching for the right word. "Strong. Like you knew you could handle anything."

The observation caught her off guard. "Thank you, sweetheart."

"Are you and Mr. Khadir dating?"

She turned off the car and considered the question. Omari was ten, but he was perceptive, and he deserved honesty appropriate to his age.

"We're getting to know each other better," she said carefully. "As friends, and maybe as something more. How would you feel about that?"

"I'd feel good about it," he said immediately. "He's nice to both of us, and he makes you smile the real way, not the pretend way."

The real way, not the pretend way. Her son saw more than she'd realized.

"Well, we're taking things slowly," she said. "And you'll always be my first priority."

"I know that." He unbuckled his seatbelt and leaned over to hug her. "But Mom? It's okay if you want to be happy too."

Later that night, after Omari was asleep, Naomi sat on her back porch with a cup of tea and let herself process the evening. The phone call with Andre had been unpleasant but clarifying. He was trying to use her relationship with Khadir as a weapon, to make her feel guilty or irresponsible.

But she didn't feel guilty. She felt hopeful.

Her phone buzzed with a text from Khadir:

> Great class tonight. Omari's grip break was textbook perfect. Hope everything is okay after your call.

She typed back:

> Everything's fine. Thank you for being so patient with both of us.

> My pleasure. Sleep well.

Simple, supportive, no demands or questions or attempts to insert himself into her drama. Just genuine care and respect for her boundaries.

She pulled the throw blanket tighter around her shoulders and looked up at the stars appearing over Sweetgum. Tomorrow she'd put on her staff badge and be Ms. Ellis again, professional and helpful and appropriately distant from parent concerns that weren't hers to handle.

But tonight, she was just Naomi—a woman learning to be strong without being hard, learning to set boundaries without building walls, learning that sometimes the best defense was knowing exactly who you were and what you deserved.

And what she deserved, she was beginning to believe, was quite a lot indeed.

CHAPTER EIGHT

K hadir was restocking gi belts when his phone buzzed with a text from Naomi:

> Quick favor? I need to stop by Nerd Central after work to pick up a graphic novel for a reluctant reader. Know anything about comics for 10-year-olds?

He smiled, typing back:

> Meet you there at 4:30? I might have some ideas.

> Perfect. See you then.

He finished organizing the equipment room and grabbed his keys. Demetrius Lakeson's comic shop was only two blocks from the dojo, an easy walk on a pleasant Thursday afternoon. But more importantly, it was a chance to see Naomi outside of their usual contexts—not at the dojo, not on a formal date, just two people running errands together.

The normalcy of it appealed to him more than it probably should.

Nerd Central occupied a narrow storefront between the florist and a tax preparation office that had been closed since April. The windows were packed with colorful displays—super-hero figurines, gaming dice, and hand-drawn signs advertising weekly tournaments. A bell chimed when Khadir pushed through the door.

"Well, well," Demetrius looked up from behind the counter where he was sorting trading cards. "The dojo master himself. What brings you to my den of geekdom?"

"Meeting someone," Khadir said. "We're looking for age-appropriate comics for a ten-year-old."

"Boy or girl?"

The bell chimed again, and Naomi stepped inside, looking slightly overwhelmed by the sheer volume of colorful merchandise packed into the small space.

"This is quite a store," she said, taking in the organized chaos of comic books, board games, and collectibles.

"Naomi Ellis," Demetrius said with a knowing grin. "Heard you were dating our resident martial arts guru."

Heat climbed up Khadir's neck. "Demetrius—"

"What? It's a small town. People talk. Plus, you two look good together." He turned back to Naomi. "So you're looking for something to hook a reluctant reader?"

"One of my students," Naomi said. "He's incredibly bright, but traditional chapter books haven't clicked for him yet. I thought maybe graphic novels..."

"Smart thinking. Visual storytelling can be a bridge to text-heavy formats." Demetrius moved from behind the counter. "What's the student interested in?"

"Science topics, especially weather phenomena," Naomi said. "He gets excited about meteorology but struggles with traditional text formats."

"Well, superheroes and weather go hand in hand. But let me show you something different first." He led them to a section labeled 'Educational Graphics.' "This series—*Science Comics.* They cover everything from dinosaurs to the solar system to—" He pulled a slim volume from the shelf. "Weather and climate."

Naomi flipped through the book, her face lighting up as she scanned the pages. "This is perfect. Look—it explains how lightning forms, different types of storms, the science behind thunder. But it's presented like a story, with characters and adventure."

"Exactly. Kids learn without realizing they're learning." Demetrius pulled out two more volumes. "Volcanoes and earthquakes, if he's into natural disasters. And this one about the solar system."

Khadir watched Naomi evaluate the books with her professional eye—checking reading levels, flipping to random pages to assess complexity, mentally cataloging how they might fit into her library's collection. Her dedication to matching the right book to the right child was evident in every careful consideration.

"These are wonderful," she said finally. "I'll take all three."

"Good choice. Kid's gonna love 'em." Demetrius rang up the purchase, then paused. "You know what, hang on a second."

He disappeared into the back room and returned with two small items—a microscope pin in bright silver and blue, and a lightning bolt pin in bright yellow and blue.

"The microscope's for your science kid," he said, setting one pin on the counter. "And the lightning bolt..." He looked at Khadir. "Didn't you mention your student has a thing for thunderstorms?"

Khadir glanced at Naomi. "If it's okay with you, I'd like to get this for Omari. He's been working so hard in class."

"He'd love it," Naomi said softly. "He wears lightning bolt socks to every class."

"Both on the house," Demetrius said with a wave of his hand. "Tell the science kid it's from a fellow weather enthusiast, and tell your lightning kid it's for good training."

Khadir felt something warm unfurl in his chest as he watched the interaction. This was Sweetgum at its best—a community that noticed and celebrated its children's interests, that went out of its way to nurture young minds.

"Thank you," Naomi said, accepting the pin with genuine gratitude. "David's going to be thrilled."

Outside the comic shop, they walked slowly toward the town square, Naomi's bag of books swinging gently between them.

"That was sweet of Demetrius," she said. "I didn't expect him to be so... grandfatherly."

"He's got a soft spot for kids, especially the ones who don't fit typical molds. Spends half his Saturdays teaching board games to middle schoolers who'd rather be here than at the mall."

"I love that. There's something special about adults who really see children as individuals, not just small versions of what they think kids should be."

They paused at the intersection of Pine and Main, and Khadir found himself reluctant to end their impromptu time together.

"Want to walk by the lake?" he asked. "I need to tape a flyer to the kiosk anyway, and it's a nice afternoon."

"That sounds perfect."

Sweetgum Lake stretched out before them, its surface reflecting the late afternoon clouds in rippling mirror images. The walking trail was busy with joggers and families with strollers, but they found a quiet spot near the information kiosk where Khadir could post his Confidence & Kindness Night flyer.

"This event is really coming together," Naomi observed, reading over his shoulder as he smoothed the tape. "Community self-defense demo, reading corner, hot chocolate. It sounds wonderful."

"I'm hoping it'll introduce more families to what we do. Sometimes people have preconceptions about martial arts—they think it's all about aggression or competition."

"And you want to show them it's about confidence and community."

"Exactly." He finished with the flyer and turned to face her. "Though I have to admit, part of me is nervous about it. What if nobody comes? What if the whole thing falls flat?"

"It won't fall flat," Naomi said with such certainty that he found himself believing her. "You're offering something people need—practical skills, community connection, a safe space for families. Trust me, they'll come."

They found a bench facing the water and settled into comfortable conversation. Naomi told him more about her student who would receive the books—a quiet boy named David who lit up during science lessons but struggled with traditional reading assignments.

"He has this incredible vocabulary when he's talking about things that interest him," she said. "But put a chapter book in front of him, and he shuts down. I think he's been told he's 'not a reader' so many times that he believes it."

"Labels can be powerful," Khadir agreed. "Good and bad. At the dojo, I try never to call anyone a 'natural' or 'uncoordinated' or anything that might stick."

"What do you call them instead?"

"Learning. Everyone's always learning, just at their own pace and in their own way."

Naomi smiled. "I like that. Mind if I steal it for the library?"

"Steal away."

A family with young children claimed the bench next to theirs, the kids immediately running toward the water while their parents called warnings about staying back from the edge.

The scene was peaceful, normal—exactly the kind of everyday moment that made Sweetgum feel like home.

"Can I ask you something?" Naomi said, her tone shifting slightly.

"Of course."

"The other night, when Andre called during class... you didn't ask what it was about. You didn't push for details or try to offer advice. That was..." She paused, searching for words. "That was exactly what I needed. But I'm curious why you held back."

Khadir considered the question. "Because it wasn't mine to fix," he said finally. "And because I figured if you wanted to talk about it, you'd bring it up yourself."

"Most people want to know. They want details, or they want to help, or they want to tell me what I should do differently."

"I'm not most people."

The simple statement hung between them, loaded with meaning. She studied his profile as he watched a jogger pass by on the trail.

"No," she said quietly. "You're not."

They sat in comfortable silence for a while, watching the lake's gentle activity. Eventually, Khadir checked his watch—a habit from his military days that had never quite faded.

"I should probably head back soon," he said. "I've got a private lesson at six."

"Of course." Naomi gathered her bag. "Thank you for the comic book consultation. And for the walk. This was nice."

"It was." He stood and offered her his hand to help her up from the bench. "Same time Saturday for your class?"

"Wouldn't miss it."

They walked back toward town together, their pace naturally slower as they approached the point where they'd part ways. Near the intersection where Naomi would turn toward the school parking lot to collect her car, Khadir slowed to a stop.

"Naomi?"

"Yes?"

"I know things are complicated right now. With your ex-husband, with Omari adjusting to everything, with us figuring out what this is." He gestured between them. "I just want you to know—there's no pressure from my end. Whatever pace feels right to you, that's the right pace."

Her expression softened. "Thank you. That means more than you probably realize."

"I realize plenty."

She rose on her toes and pressed a quick kiss to his cheek—nothing dramatic, just a sweet gesture that sent warmth radiating through his chest.

"See you Saturday," she said, then walked toward her car with a lightness in her step that made him smile.

Khadir headed back to the dojo, the memory of that brief kiss lingering on his skin. As he unlocked the front door and flipped on the lights, he found himself looking forward to Saturday with an anticipation that had nothing to do with martial arts instruction and everything to do with simply being in the same space as Naomi Ellis.

His phone buzzed with a text:

> David loved the science books and pin! And Omari hasn't stopped grinning since he saw the lightning bolt. You and Demetrius made both boys' week. Thank you. - N

He typed back:

> Tell David it's from one science enthusiast to another, and tell Omari it's for all his hard work. Sweet dreams.

> You too.

Simple exchanges that felt like small gifts. This was what he'd been waiting for without fully realizing it—not grand romantic gestures or dramatic declarations, but the quiet pleasure of someone thinking to share their child's joy with him, the easy intimacy of goodnight texts, the knowledge that he was becoming part of their daily life in small, meaningful ways.

As he prepared for his evening lesson, Khadir found himself humming under his breath, more content than he'd been in years. Good things, it turned out, really did come to those who were patient enough to recognize them when they arrived.

CHAPTER NINE

The dojo had been transformed. Where the usual training equipment normally sat, colorful mats now formed a large demonstration area surrounded by folding chairs. In one corner, Naomi had created a cozy reading nook with low bookshelves, floor cushions, and a hand-painted sign that read "Books About Courage." The air smelled of Mrs. Zhang's homemade hot chocolate, which simmered in two large thermoses on a table near the entrance.

Naomi adjusted a display of picture books for the third time, her stomach fluttering with nervous energy. She'd arrived an hour early to set up the reading corner, and now families were beginning to filter through the front door—parents looking curious and slightly uncertain, children wide-eyed at the transformation of the familiar space.

"It looks perfect," Khadir said, appearing beside her with two paper cups of hot chocolate. "The reading corner was exactly what this event needed."

"I hope so. I keep second-guessing my book selections." She accepted the cup gratefully, letting the warmth steady her hands. "What if parents think some of these are too advanced? What if the younger kids get bored?"

"Then they'll find something else to do, and that's okay too." His voice carried the calm confidence she'd come to rely on. "This isn't a test, Naomi. It's just neighbors getting to know neighbors."

She took a sip of the hot chocolate and felt some of her tension ease. Mrs. Zhang had outdone herself—the drink was rich and warming, with hints of cinnamon and vanilla that made the whole dojo feel festive.

More families arrived: the Thompsons with both their daughters, the Martinez family with their energetic twin boys, several parents Naomi recognized from school pickup but didn't know well. Near the door, Omari was helping Kiana greet newcomers, his confidence evident in the way he stood straight and made eye contact when introducing himself.

"Welcome, everyone!" Khadir called the group to attention once about twenty people had gathered. "I'm Khadir Grant, and this is Kiana Wilson. We're so glad you're here tonight."

He looked comfortable in front of the group, Naomi noticed. Not performing or putting on a show, just genuinely pleased to share something he cared about.

"Tonight is about two things," he continued. "Confidence and kindness. They might seem like opposite qualities, but they're actually partners. Real confidence comes from knowing you can take care of yourself and the people you love. And real kindness comes from having the security to be generous with others."

A few parents nodded, and Naomi saw some of the initial skepticism on faces beginning to soften.

"We're going to show you some basic techniques—nothing aggressive, nothing designed to hurt anyone. Just simple skills that help you create space, stay safe, and move through the world with more assurance."

Kiana stepped forward. "And while the adults are learning,

the kids can explore our reading corner, where Ms. Naomi has collected some wonderful books about courage, friendship, and standing up for what's right."

Several children immediately gravitated toward the books, drawn by the colorful covers and comfortable seating. Naomi felt a flutter of pride as she watched a shy girl pick up one of her carefully selected picture books.

"Let's start with something everyone can do," Khadir said, moving to the center of the mat. "It's called situational awareness, and it's your first and best defense in any situation."

He had the group practice simple exercises—scanning their environment, identifying exits, paying attention to their instincts about people and places. Nothing dramatic or frightening, just practical skills presented as common sense.

"Your gut feelings matter," he told them. "If something feels off, trust that feeling. If someone makes you uncomfortable, you don't have to be polite about it. Your safety is more important than social niceness."

Naomi found herself nodding along. How many times had she ignored her instincts about Andre's behavior because she didn't want to seem unreasonable? How many red flags had she explained away in the name of being a good partner?

Next, Khadir demonstrated basic boundary-setting techniques—how to stand with confidence, how to use your voice effectively, how to create physical distance without seeming aggressive.

"Boundaries aren't mean," he said. "They're kind—to yourself and to others. They let everyone know what to expect."

In the reading corner, more children had settled in with books. Naomi noticed Omari showing the lightning pin Demetrius had given him to another boy, both of them poring over one of the weather-themed graphic novels she'd selected.

"Now we'll try some physical techniques," Khadir said.

"Remember, these aren't about fighting or hurting anyone. They're about creating distance and getting to safety."

He and Kiana demonstrated the same basic skills Naomi and Omari had been learning—break-falls, technical stand-ups, simple grip breaks. But presented to this mixed group, the techniques took on a different quality. They looked less like martial arts and more like practical life skills.

"Mrs. Ellis," Khadir called, making her stomach jump. "Would you mind helping us demonstrate?"

She set down her hot chocolate and joined him on the mat, acutely aware of all the watching faces. Some of these parents knew her as the school librarian, others as Omari's mom. None of them had seen her in this context before.

"Naomi has been training with us for a few weeks," Khadir said. "She's going to show you how these techniques look when someone's still learning—because that's where most of us are most of the time."

He guided her through a basic sequence—someone grabbing her wrist, her breaking free, creating distance, getting back to her feet with intention. She was nervous at first, but Khadir's calm presence and the supportive atmosphere of the group helped her settle into the movements.

When she successfully completed the demonstration, spontaneous applause broke out from the watching parents. Her cheeks flushed with pride and embarrassment.

"Beautiful work," Khadir said quietly, just for her. "You looked confident and controlled."

"I felt confident," she realized with surprise. "Even with everyone watching."

The evening continued with more demonstrations and opportunities for families to try basic techniques. The atmosphere was relaxed and encouraging—parents laughing as they attempted new movements, children cheering for their adults, everyone learning together.

During a break for more hot chocolate, Mrs. Martinez approached Naomi at the reading corner.

"This is wonderful," she said, gesturing to the book display. "My son Carlos has been struggling with reading confidence, and I think these visual books might be perfect for him."

"Please, take a few home," Naomi said. "That's what they're here for."

"Are you a teacher?"

"I'm the children's librarian at Sweetgum Elementary. I love matching kids with books that spark their interest."

"Well, you've definitely sparked Carlos's interest. He's been sitting with that volcano book for twenty minutes."

More parents approached with questions about the books, about reading programs at the school, about resources for reluctant readers. Naomi found herself in her element, discussing different authors and series, recommending specific titles based on children's interests and reading levels.

Near the end of the evening, Khadir called everyone together for a final demonstration.

"We'd like to show you something special," he said. "Omari Ellis has been one of our most dedicated young students, and he's going to demonstrate the technical stand-up—getting to your feet with purpose and control."

Omari walked to the center of the mat, and Naomi held her breath. This was his moment, his chance to show what he'd learned.

He settled onto the mat, then moved through the sequence with careful precision—posting his hand, bringing his foot up, rising with controlled balance. When he reached his feet, he stood tall and proud, and the applause that followed was genuine and enthusiastic.

"That," Khadir said, "is what confidence looks like. Not aggressive, not showy, just sure. Sure of his abilities, sure of his worth, sure that he can handle whatever comes his way."

Naomi's eyes filled with tears as she watched her son bow to the applauding group. Three weeks ago, he'd been a boy who flinched at loud noises and hunched his shoulders against the world. Tonight, he stood straight and smiled at a room full of people celebrating his achievement.

As families began to pack up and say their goodbyes, several parents approached Khadir about signing up for regular classes. Others asked Naomi about book clubs or reading programs. The evening had accomplished exactly what they'd hoped—introducing the community to a different way of thinking about strength and safety.

"Thank you," Mrs. Thompson said as she collected her daughters and a small stack of books. "This was exactly what our family needed. Sarah has been having some trouble with a classmate, and I think these skills will help her feel more empowered."

After the last family left, Naomi, Khadir, Kiana, and Omari worked together to clean up the space. The easy teamwork felt natural, familial even.

"That was amazing," Kiana said as she folded the last chair. "I think we'll see at least half those families in regular classes."

"The reading corner was perfect," Khadir added. "It made the whole event feel more approachable, more family-friendly."

"I loved seeing the kids get excited about the books," Naomi said. "And the parents asking questions about reading programs—it felt like we were building something bigger than just self-defense classes."

"We were," Khadir said. "We were building community."

As they finished cleaning up, Omari yawned hugely, the excitement of the evening finally catching up with him.

"Time to get you home, buddy," Naomi said.

"Can I help clean up next time too?" he asked. "I liked being part of the team."

"Of course you can," Khadir said. "Good teammates stick together."

Outside, the October air was crisp and clear, full of the promise of changing seasons. Naomi loaded the remaining books into her car while Omari climbed into the backseat, still chattering about the evening's success.

"Naomi," Khadir called softly as she closed the trunk.

She turned to find him standing close, his expression warm and proud and something deeper.

"Thank you," he said. "For making tonight possible. For trusting me with this. For..." He paused, seeming to search for words. "For being exactly who you are."

The sincerity in his voice made her breath catch. "Thank you for including us. For making us part of something beautiful."

They stood looking at each other in the parking lot, the space between them charged with possibility and affection and the comfortable intimacy that had been building between them.

"Naomi?" he said quietly.

"Yes?"

"Would it be okay if I kissed you goodnight? Really kissed you this time?"

Her answer was to step closer, tilting her face up toward his. "I'd like that very much."

This kiss was different from their first tentative connection on the town square bench. This one was warm and sure and full of promise, the kind of kiss that spoke of feelings acknowledged and futures imagined. When they finally broke apart, they stayed close, foreheads touching.

"Goodnight," she whispered.

"Goodnight. Sweet dreams."

As she drove home with Omari dozing in the backseat, Naomi felt a deep sense of contentment settle over her. Tonight had been about confidence and kindness, about community and connection. But more than that, it had been about possibility—

the possibility of being part of something larger than herself, the possibility of love that supported rather than diminished, the possibility of a future built on mutual respect and shared values.

At the next red light, she caught her reflection in the rearview mirror and smiled. She looked like a woman who knew her own worth, who had something beautiful to look forward to, who was exactly where she was meant to be.

For the first time in years, that felt like more than enough. It felt like everything.

CHAPTER TEN

Khadir slipped the envelope under the front desk before anyone arrived Tuesday morning. Inside was enough money to cover three months of classes for the Rodriguez family—Maria had mentioned during Confidence & Kindness Night that her son Miguel wanted to join but money was tight after her husband's hours got cut at the plant.

He didn't put his name on the envelope. Just wrote "Anonymous scholarship—use as needed" in block letters and tucked it where Kiana would find it when she opened up.

Some things were better done quietly.

By Thursday, Miguel Rodriguez was bowing onto the mat with the other kids, his face bright with excitement as Kiana showed him the basic stances. His mother had tears in her eyes when she thanked "whoever made this possible," and Khadir just smiled and suggested Miguel seemed like a natural athlete.

The truth was, he'd been setting aside money for exactly this purpose since opening the dojo. Too many good kids missed out on opportunities because their parents couldn't stretch the budget to cover extras. If he could quietly bridge that gap for a few families, the dojo's mission felt more complete.

"You're humming," Kiana observed Friday afternoon as they prepared for the evening classes.

"Am I?"

"Mmm-hmm. Same tune you've been humming all week. Ever since Confidence & Kindness Night." She grinned. "It's very... satisfied humming."

Heat climbed up his neck. "I don't hum."

"You absolutely hum. And you've been doing this little smile thing when you think nobody's looking." She demonstrated an expression that was probably more dopey than he wanted to admit. "Very cute. Very 'I kissed a beautiful woman and she kissed me back.'"

"Kiana—"

"Don't even try to deny it. Half the town saw you two in the parking lot after the event. Mrs. Patterson told Mrs. Zhang, who told my grandmother, who called to ask if you needed any relationship advice from someone who's been married for fifty-three years."

Khadir rubbed his forehead. Small towns had their advantages, but privacy wasn't one of them.

"What did you tell your grandmother?"

"That you seemed to be handling things just fine on your own." Kiana's expression softened. "She's happy for you, by the way. Says it's about time you found someone worthy of all that patience you've been storing up."

Before he could respond to that uncomfortable insight, the door chimed and Naomi appeared with Omari. Her smile when she spotted Khadir was warm and genuine, and he felt that familiar flutter of anticipation in his chest.

"How was everyone's week?" he asked as they approached.

"Good," Omari said, bouncing slightly on his toes. "I used the grip break at school when Tommy grabbed my backpack. He let go right away, and I didn't have to get loud or anything."

"Perfect application," Khadir said, pride evident in his voice.

"You created space and resolved the situation without escalation."

"Mrs. Rivera said I handled it like a champion."

"She was right."

Naomi caught his eye over Omari's head, her expression full of quiet gratitude. Three weeks ago, a backpack-grabbing incident would have sent her son into tears and anxiety. Now he was problem-solving and advocating for himself with calm confidence.

"Adults tonight?" Khadir asked as Omari ran off to join the other kids.

"Definitely. Though I have to warn you, I might be a little distracted." She gestured toward her phone. "We got some great news at school today, and I'm still processing it."

"Good news, I hope?"

"The best. Remember that reluctant reader I mentioned? David, who I bought the science books for?"

Khadir nodded.

"He read all three graphic novels in two days, then came to the library asking for more. Today he checked out his first chapter book—something about storm chasers. His teacher says he's been writing in his journal about weather phenomena during free writing time."

The joy in her voice made Khadir's chest warm. "That's incredible."

"It really is. There's nothing like watching a child discover they love something they thought they couldn't do." She paused, then added quietly, "Kind of like adults discovering they're stronger than they knew."

The comment held layers of meaning, and Khadir found himself studying her face. She looked different than she had three weeks ago—more settled, more confident in her own skin. The constant tension around her eyes had eased, and she moved with more assurance.

"Speaking of which," he said, "how do you feel about learning something new tonight?"

"Nervous and excited, which seems to be my default state lately."

They worked through warm-ups, then moved into reviewing the techniques she'd been mastering. Her hip escapes were smooth now, her technical stand-ups controlled and confident. She'd developed what martial artists called "good base"—that sense of knowing where her body was in space, how to move with intention instead of just reaction.

"Tonight we're adding something called transition flows," Khadir explained. "Instead of learning techniques in isolation, we're going to connect them. Hip escape to technical stand-up to ready position. One movement flowing into the next."

He demonstrated the sequence, his movements economical and precise. Then he guided Naomi through it slowly, his hands on her shoulders to help her feel the rhythm.

"Don't think about each technique separately," he coached. "Think about the whole flow. Like a conversation where each sentence leads naturally to the next."

She tried it tentatively at first, then with growing confidence. By the third repetition, the movements were starting to connect, her body finding the natural transitions between positions.

"That felt..." she paused, searching for words. "Like dancing, almost. But useful dancing."

"That's exactly right. The best martial arts feels like that—purposeful movement that's also beautiful."

They worked through several variations of the flow, and Khadir found himself impressed by how quickly she adapted. Some students took months to develop the kind of body awareness she was showing after just a few weeks.

"You're a natural at this," he said during a water break.

"I don't feel like a natural. I feel like someone who's finally learning to pay attention to what her body's trying to tell her."

The comment made him pause. "What do you mean?"

"For years, I ignored my physical instincts. If something felt wrong, I talked myself out of trusting that feeling. If someone made me uncomfortable, I told myself I was being too sensitive." She took a sip of water. "This training is teaching me to trust those instincts again. To believe my body knows things my mind hasn't figured out yet."

Khadir nodded slowly. "That's one of the most important lessons. Your intuition is information. It deserves attention."

"Andre used to tell me I was 'too reactive,' that I needed to 'think more and feel less.'" She shook her head. "Turns out feeling more and trusting those feelings was exactly what I needed to do."

The mention of her ex-husband sent a familiar tightness through Khadir's jaw, but he kept his expression neutral. These insights were hers to have, her healing to process. His job was to provide a safe space for that growth, not to insert his own anger about how she'd been treated.

They finished class with stretching and confidence logs. Naomi wrote,

Learned to flow instead of just react.

And when she handed it to him, their fingers brushed in the exchange that had become familiar and anticipated.

"Same time Saturday?" she asked as they gathered their things.

"Actually," Khadir said, "I was wondering if you and Omari might want to celebrate something tomorrow instead."

"Celebrate what?"

"Miguel Rodriguez getting his first stripe tomorrow. Kiana

and I usually take new stripe students for ice cream after class. Thought you two might like to join us—if you're free."

Naomi's face lit up. "I'd love that. Omari will be thrilled. He's been asking when he might earn his first stripe."

"Soon," Khadir said. "He's close. Maybe another week or two."

Outside, the October evening was crisp and clear, full of the promise of changing seasons. As Naomi loaded her gym bag into the car, Khadir found himself reluctant to end their time together.

"Naomi?"

She turned, eyebrows raised in question.

"I'm glad you're learning to trust your instincts again."

"Me too." She smiled. "They seem to be leading me in good directions these days."

As he watched her drive away, Khadir felt that familiar sense of contentment settle over him. The anonymous scholarship, Naomi's growing confidence, Omari's continued progress, the prospect of ice cream and easy conversation tomorrow—these were the moments that made everything worthwhile.

His phone buzzed with a text:

Thank you for tonight. Looking forward to celebrating Miguel tomorrow. Sweet dreams. - N

He typed back:

My pleasure. See you at 4. Sleep well.

Walking to his car, Khadir realized Kiana was right—he was humming. Something light and hopeful that matched the rhythm of his footsteps on the pavement.

Some weeks, everything fell into place exactly as it should. This was turning out to be one of those weeks.

Saturday afternoon at Scoop! There It Is! was exactly as chaotic and joyful as ice cream with excited children should be. Miguel Rodriguez wore his new stripe with obvious pride, and his mother Maria beamed as she watched him demonstrate his improved break-fall technique for anyone who would pay attention.

"Two scoops," Miguel announced when it was his turn to order. "Chocolate and strawberry. With sprinkles."

"It's a celebration," Kiana said with a grin. "Sprinkles are mandatory."

Omari ordered his usual—vanilla with chocolate chips—but added rainbow sprinkles in honor of Miguel's achievement. The gesture was small but thoughtful, exactly the kind of inclusive kindness that made Khadir proud of the community they were building at the dojo.

They claimed a large table near the window, and the conversation flowed easily between English and Spanish as Maria shared stories about Miguel's newfound confidence at school.

"Before the dojo, he was so shy," she said, switching back to English so everyone could follow. "Now he stands up straight, makes eye contact. His teacher says he's a different child."

"Same child," Khadir corrected gently. "Just one who knows his own worth now."

Naomi caught his eye across the table and smiled. They'd had similar conversations about Omari, about the way confidence changed not just behavior but posture, presence, the way a child moved through the world.

"Mr. Khadir," Miguel said, chocolate ice cream smudged on his chin, "when do I get to learn the cool spinning thing that Omari does?"

"The technical stand-up?" Khadir asked. "Soon. First you

need to master your break-falls and hip escapes. Foundation comes before fancy moves."

"Everything builds on everything else," Omari added sagely, clearly repeating something he'd heard in class.

"Exactly right."

As they finished their ice cream, other community members stopped by to chat. Mrs. Zhang from the Chinese restaurant complimented Miguel on his stripe and asked about upcoming classes. Mr. Peterson from the hardware store mentioned he'd been thinking about joining the adult program since Confidence & Kindness Night.

"Word's getting around town," Kiana observed quietly to Khadir. "Good word."

Indeed, the dojo's reputation was growing in exactly the way he'd hoped—not as a place for tough guys to learn fighting, but as a community resource for building confidence and practical life skills. The kind of place parents felt good about bringing their children, where families could learn together.

As they prepared to leave, Maria pulled Khadir aside.

"I don't know how to thank whoever made Miguel's scholarship possible," she said, her voice thick with emotion. "These classes... they're changing his life."

"No thanks necessary," Khadir said. "Miguel earned his place here through hard work and dedication. That's all that matters."

"Still, if you ever find out who it was, please tell them..." She paused, searching for words. "Tell them they gave a mother her son back. The confident, happy boy he was always meant to be."

Outside the ice cream shop, families began parting ways for the evening. Miguel hugged everyone goodbye, his stripe-wearing gi tied carefully around his waist like a badge of honor.

"That was wonderful," Naomi said as she and Omari prepared to head home. "Miguel's so proud, and seeing his mother's joy..."

"These are my favorite parts," Khadir admitted. "Not the

techniques or the physical skills, but watching kids discover they're capable of more than they knew."

"And watching parents discover the same thing about themselves," she added, her meaning clear.

As Omari climbed into the backseat, chattering about ice cream flavors and stripe requirements, Khadir found himself stepping closer to Naomi.

"I had a good time today," he said.

"Me too. It felt like..." She paused, seeming to consider her words. "Like family. The kind of community celebration I want Omari to grow up with."

"He's lucky to have you as his mom."

"I'm lucky to have found this place. Found you." The words came out quietly, but with conviction. "Both of us are."

They stood looking at each other in the afternoon light, and Khadir felt the truth of what she'd said settle deep in his chest. Luck, yes, but also something more deliberate. Choices made with care, patience rewarded, two people brave enough to trust what was growing between them.

"See you Thursday," she said, rising on her toes to press a quick kiss to his cheek.

"Looking forward to it."

As he watched them drive away, Khadir reflected on the afternoon. Anonymous scholarships, stripe celebrations, community connections, the easy intimacy of shared ice cream and comfortable conversation. These were the building blocks of the life he'd been hoping for without fully realizing it—not grand gestures or dramatic moments, but the quiet accumulation of meaningful experiences with people who mattered.

His phone buzzed:

> Omari wants to know if you think he's ready for his stripe test next week. I told him that's your call, but he's been practicing his sequences all afternoon. - N

He typed back:

> Tell him I think he's almost ready. Maybe one more week of solid practice. Good things are worth waiting for.

> He says he can wait. Patience is part of confidence, right?

> Exactly right. Sweet dreams to both of you.

> You too.

Walking to his car, Khadir found himself humming again—that same hopeful tune Kiana had caught him with all week. The sound of a man whose patience was finally being rewarded, whose careful investment in community and relationships was paying dividends in ways both small and profound.

Some celebrations were loud and public. But the best ones, he was learning, were quiet and shared with exactly the right people at exactly the right time.

CHAPTER ELEVEN

Justin Time's Clock and Watch Repair occupied a narrow storefront that somehow managed to feel both cramped and cozy. Vintage timepieces lined the walls in careful rows, their steady ticking creating a symphony of overlapping rhythms that most people found either soothing or maddening. Khadir had always found it peaceful.

"She should be ready in about twenty minutes," Justin Clark said, examining the delicate gold watch Khadir had brought in. "Just needs a new strap and a good cleaning. Your mother had excellent taste—this is a beautiful piece."

"Thank you for working her in so quickly."

"No problem. I know how it is with family heirlooms." Justin bent over his workbench, already absorbed in the precise work of watch repair. "You can wait here if you want, or walk around town and come back."

Khadir checked the time on the wall clock—a grandfather clock Justin had restored himself, all rich wood and brass fittings. "I think I'll take a walk. Maybe grab some tea at Roasted Beans."

"Sounds good. See you in twenty."

The October afternoon was crisp and bright, perfect weather for wandering Pine Street and thinking. Khadir had been carrying his mother's watch in his dresser drawer for two years, telling himself he'd get it fixed someday. Today felt like the right someday, though he couldn't put his finger on exactly why.

Maybe because everything else in his life was finally falling into place. The dojo was thriving, his community relationships were strong, and Naomi... well, Naomi was becoming something he'd stopped hoping for and started building toward.

Roasted Beans was moderately busy for a Tuesday afternoon —the usual mix of college students with laptops, retirees sharing coffee and gossip, and workers grabbing late-day caffeine fixes. Joanne waved from behind the counter as he approached.

"Let me guess," she said, already reaching for the mint tea. "Large, to go?"

"Actually, make it for here today. I'm waiting for something at Justin's and have some time to kill."

"Waiting for what?" The question came from behind him, and he turned to find Naomi approaching with a small stack of flyers in her hand.

"My mother's watch," he said, surprised and pleased to see her. "Justin's fixing the strap. What brings you to town on a Tuesday afternoon?"

"Posting flyers for the school's fall book fair." She held up the colorful announcements. "Joanne lets me put them on the community board in exchange for occasional help organizing events."

"Smart business relationship."

"I like to think so." She ordered her usual coffee—something complicated with extra foam that Joanne made with practiced ease. "Mind if I sit with you while you wait? I'm ahead of schedule, and the company would be nice."

"Please."

They found a table by the window, and Khadir watched Naomi settle into her chair with the unconscious confidence that had become natural to her over the past weeks. The change wasn't dramatic—she'd always been graceful—but there was a new quality to her movements. More assured, less apologetic for taking up space.

"How was your day?" he asked.

"Good, actually. Really good." Her face lit up with enthusiasm. "Remember that reluctant reader I mentioned? David?"

"The one who discovered graphic novels."

"He finished his first chapter book yesterday and immediately checked out two more. His teacher says he's been writing stories during free time—weather adventure stories with kids as the main characters." She stirred her coffee, still smiling. "There's nothing quite like watching a child discover they love something they thought was impossible."

"Sounds familiar," Khadir said.

"What do you mean?"

"Adults discovering they're stronger than they knew. Kids finding confidence they didn't know they had. Parents learning to trust their instincts again." He met her eyes across the table. "Transformation isn't just for reluctant readers."

A flush of pleasure crossed her features. "I suppose you're right. Though I have to say, the book victories feel a little more straightforward than the life ones."

"How so?"

She considered the question, absently turning her coffee cup in its saucer. "With books, I can see exactly what a child needs and find the perfect match. This author for the kid who loves adventure, that series for the one who needs to see herself reflected in the story. It's problem-solving with clear solutions."

"And life problems don't have clear solutions?"

"Not the important ones, no. Like figuring out how to co-parent with someone who sees every boundary as a personal attack. Or knowing when it's okay to let yourself care about someone new." She paused, seeming to realize what she'd revealed. "Sorry. That got more personal than I intended."

"Don't apologize. I asked."

They sat in comfortable silence for a moment, watching the afternoon foot traffic through the window. Khadir found himself studying Naomi's profile, noting the way afternoon light caught the natural curl of her hair, the determined set of her jaw when she was thinking through something complicated.

"Can I ask you something?" she said eventually.

"Always."

"What made you decide to fix your mother's watch today? You mentioned you'd been meaning to do it for a while."

The question caught him off guard, partly because he wasn't sure he had a good answer.

"Honestly? I'm not entirely sure. This morning I was getting dressed and saw it sitting in my dresser drawer, and it felt like... like it was time." He paused, trying to articulate something he hadn't fully examined himself. "Maybe because things feel more settled now. More permanent. Like I'm finally building the life I want instead of just maintaining the one I ended up with."

"That's a beautiful way to put it."

"What about you? Are you building the life you want?"

She tilted her head, considering. "I'm starting to. For so long, I was just trying to survive each day, get through each challenge, keep Omari safe and happy while managing Andre's... intensity. I wasn't thinking about what I actually wanted—just what I needed to avoid."

"And now?"

"Now I'm starting to think about what I want to move toward instead of just what I want to move away from." She met his eyes. "It's scarier than I expected, wanting things again. Hoping for things."

"What kinds of things?"

The question hung between them, loaded with possibility and risk. Khadir could see Naomi weighing how much to reveal, how vulnerable to let herself be.

"Partnership that feels like teamwork instead of management," she said finally. "The kind of relationship where both people become better versions of themselves, not smaller ones. A community where Omari can grow up seeing healthy examples of love and respect." She paused. "Family traditions that aren't built around walking on eggshells."

Her voice grew quiet on the last part, and Khadir felt a familiar anger toward her ex-husband flare in his chest. But this wasn't the time for his protective instincts—this was the time for listening.

"Those sound like very reasonable things to want," he said.

"Do they? Sometimes I wonder if I'm asking for too much. If I should just be grateful that Omari and I are safe and stable, and not hope for more than that."

"Naomi." He waited until she looked at him. "Wanting love and partnership and joy—that's not asking for too much. That's asking for what you deserve."

Her eyes filled with tears, but she blinked them back. "It's been a long time since someone told me what I deserve instead of what I should be grateful for."

Before Khadir could respond, his phone chimed with a text from Justin:

> Watch is ready whenever you want to pick it up.

"That's my cue," he said, showing her the message. "Want to walk with me? You could post your flyers on the way."

"I'd like that."

They left Roasted Beans together, and Naomi made quick stops to post book fair flyers at the florist, the insurance office, and the small grocery store. At each location, she was greeted warmly—clearly she'd built genuine relationships throughout the community over her years of living in Sweetgum.

"You know everyone," Khadir observed as they headed toward Justin's shop.

"Small town advantage. Also small town disadvantage, depending on the situation." She glanced at him sideways. "Everyone's going to know we had coffee together within an hour."

"Does that bother you?"

"Not anymore. A month ago, maybe. I was so worried about Andre using every interaction as ammunition." She shrugged. "But I realized I can't live my life trying to avoid his criticism. He's going to find fault no matter what I do."

At Justin's shop, they stepped back into the symphony of ticking timepieces. Justin looked up from his workbench with a satisfied expression.

"Perfect timing," he said, holding up the restored watch. "Good as new. Actually, better than new—the old strap was completely shot."

Khadir accepted the watch, noting how the gold gleamed after Justin's careful cleaning, how the new leather strap made the whole piece look elegant and timeless.

"She's beautiful," Naomi said softly, admiring the delicate face with its tiny diamonds marking the hours.

"My mother wore it every day for thirty years," Khadir said. "Even when she was sick, even when she couldn't remember our names, she'd ask for her watch."

"You must miss her."

"I do. But having this..." He fastened the watch around his wrist, noting how right it felt. "It's like carrying a piece of her with me. The good parts. The love and strength and grace."

"That's exactly what family heirlooms should be," Naomi said. "Reminders of the best in the people who came before us."

They thanked Justin and stepped back onto the sidewalk. The afternoon was growing later, shadows lengthening as evening approached.

"I should probably head home," Naomi said. "Omari has homework, and I promised we'd work on his stripe requirements tonight."

"Of course. Thanks for keeping me company while I waited."

"Thanks for letting me. It was..." She paused, searching for words. "It was the kind of afternoon I want to have more of. Easy conversation, shared time, no drama or crisis management required."

"Just normal life."

"Just normal life," she agreed. "Which feels pretty extraordinary after the last few years."

They walked toward their cars, and Khadir found himself reluctant to end their time together. The conversation at Roasted Beans had felt significant—not because of any dramatic revelations, but because of the quiet intimacy of shared hopes and honest vulnerability.

When they reached Naomi's car, she turned to face him.

"Khadir?"

"Yes?"

"Thank you for listening today. For not trying to fix anything or offer solutions to problems you can't solve. For just... hearing me."

"Thank you for trusting me with it."

She rose on her toes and kissed him—not the quick goodbye peck he'd been expecting, but something deeper, more intentional. When they broke apart, they stayed close for a moment, foreheads almost touching.

"I should go," she whispered.

"I know."

"See you Thursday?"

"Looking forward to it."

As he watched her drive away, Khadir looked down at his mother's watch on his wrist. The afternoon light caught the gold face, and he could almost hear his mother's voice: *Good things come to those who know their worth and aren't afraid to wait for what they deserve.*

His phone buzzed with a text from Naomi:

> Thank you for a perfect unexpected afternoon. Sweet dreams when bedtime comes. - N

He typed back:

> Thank you for making ordinary moments feel special. Sleep well.

> You too.

Walking to his own car, Khadir felt that familiar sense of rightness he'd been experiencing more and more lately. Not the dramatic rush of new romance, but the deeper satisfaction of building something real with someone who understood both patience and partnership.

His mother's watch ticked steadily against his wrist, marking time with the same reliability she'd shown throughout her life. Some things, he reflected, were worth waiting for. Some people were worth the careful investment of hope and patience.

And some afternoons, like this one, reminded you that the best parts of life often came disguised as ordinary moments shared with exactly the right person.

CHAPTER TWELVE

Thursday's class focused on what Khadir called "gentle exits"—techniques for creating distance and getting away from unwanted contact without causing injury.

"The goal is always de-escalation," he explained to the mixed group of adults and older teens. "We're not trying to hurt anyone. We're trying to get safe and get away."

He demonstrated a grip break, showing how to peel someone's fingers away from your wrist using leverage instead of force. The movement was smooth and controlled, almost gentle despite its effectiveness.

"This works because we're not fighting against their strength," he said. "We're finding the mechanical weakness in their grip and using physics to our advantage."

Naomi partnered with Mrs. Rodriguez for the drill, both women working through the technique methodically. After three weeks of regular classes, the movements were becoming second nature to Naomi—her body remembering the angles and timing without her conscious mind having to direct every motion.

"Beautiful work," Khadir said, observing their practice.

"Remember, the moment you create that opening, you move. Don't hesitate, don't negotiate. Distance first, everything else second."

As they moved through variations of the grip break, Naomi found herself thinking about the concept of gentle exits in contexts beyond physical self-defense. How many conversations with Andre could have been resolved more easily if she'd known how to create distance without escalation? How many situations had she stayed trapped in simply because she didn't know there were ways to leave that didn't require drama or confrontation?

After class, as other students filtered out, Khadir approached her with a slight smile.

"You looked thoughtful during the grip break drills," he observed. "More than usual, I mean."

"I was thinking about applications," she said. "How the same principles might work in other situations."

"Such as?"

"Difficult conversations. Situations where someone's trying to control the interaction and you need to get out without making things worse."

Khadir nodded slowly. "The beauty of these techniques is that they work on multiple levels. Physical, emotional, psychological. It's all about recognizing when someone's trying to control you and having tools to respond."

"I wish I'd learned this years ago."

"You learned it when you were ready to learn it," he said gently. "Sometimes we need to be in the right place mentally before we can absorb certain lessons."

As they packed up their gear, Kiana called from the front desk. "Khadir? Tia's here for her aunt's class next door. She wants to know if she can borrow you for something."

Through the front windows, they could see Lights, Camera, Dance studio next door, where Sean Martin was teaching an evening class to a group of middle schoolers. A small girl with braided pigtails was gesturing animatedly near the entrance.

"What does she need?" Khadir asked.

"Something about a fundraiser video? She seems pretty excited about it."

Khadir and Naomi exchanged glances. "Want to see what this is about?" he asked.

"I'm curious now."

They stepped outside and were immediately approached by Tia, Sean's seven-year-old niece, who bounced on her toes with barely contained energy.

"Mr. Khadir! Ms. Naomi!" she called. "Uncle Sean said I could ask if you want to be in our video!"

"What kind of video?" Naomi asked, crouching down to Tia's level.

"We're making a commercial for the youth center fundraiser. Uncle Sean says we need people from different parts of town to show how everyone supports the kids." She looked between them hopefully. "We just need you to sway a little bit with the music. Like two minutes, max."

Sean appeared in the doorway, looking slightly embarrassed. "Sorry, guys. She's been planning this all week. I told her you might be too busy—"

"We can do two minutes of swaying," Khadir said, surprising himself. "Right, Naomi?"

"Absolutely. What do we need to do?"

What followed was perhaps the most ridiculous and delightful ten minutes of Naomi's week. Tia positioned them in front of the dance studio's mirrors while Sean cued up a gentle instrumental track. The "choreography" consisted of nothing more than swaying side to side, occasionally raising their joined hands, and smiling at the camera.

"More smiling!" Tia directed from behind her tablet. "This is supposed to show that Sweetgum is a happy place!"

"I think my face is going to cramp," Naomi whispered to Khadir as they swayed through another take.

"Almost done," he whispered back. "Though I have to say, you're a natural at this."

"I teach elementary school. I'm used to performing enthusiasm on command."

When Tia finally declared the video perfect, they were both laughing and slightly out of breath despite the minimal physical demands.

"Thank you so much!" Tia threw her arms around both their legs simultaneously. "This is going to be the best fundraiser video ever!"

"I'm sure it will be," Naomi said, returning the little girl's hug.

As they walked back toward the dojo, Khadir shook his head with amusement. "I can honestly say I never expected to end up in a fundraiser video when I got up this morning."

"Life in a small town," Naomi said. "You never know when you'll be recruited for community service."

"Do you mind? The recruiting, I mean."

"Not anymore. There was a time when any unexpected request would send me into panic mode—what if Andre found out, what if he used it against me somehow, what if I wasn't good enough at whatever was being asked." She paused. "Now it just feels like being part of something bigger than myself."

"That's a big shift."

"It really is. And it's not just about Andre being out of the picture. It's about..." She searched for words. "About feeling like I belong somewhere again. Like I have something to contribute beyond just surviving each day."

They'd reached their cars, but neither made a move to leave. The evening air was crisp and comfortable, and the shared silliness of the video had created a bubble of lighthearted intimacy around them.

"I keep meaning to ask," Khadir said, "how are things with Omari's situation at school? Any more incidents?"

"Actually, things have been much better. He had another interaction with Marcus last week—something about a pencil—but Omari just moved to a different seat and kept working. No drama, no big emotional reaction, just problem-solving." Pride was evident in her voice. "Mrs. Rivera says his confidence has transformed the dynamic completely."

"Bullies look for easy targets," Khadir said. "When someone stops being an easy target, the bullies usually move on to someone else."

"Which is its own kind of sad, isn't it? That there's always someone else."

"It is. But changing the whole system starts with individual kids learning they don't have to be victims. Omari's learning that lesson."

"Thanks to you."

"Thanks to him. And to you. I just provided some tools." Khadir leaned against his car, making no move to get in. "He's been asking about his stripe test."

"Every day. I think he's more excited about earning it than he was about his birthday last year."

"He's ready. His break-falls are solid, his technical stand-ups are clean, and his attitude is exactly what we look for in students moving to the next level."

"When were you thinking?"

"Next Thursday, maybe? If he's ready, if you're comfortable with it."

Naomi's face lit up. "He's going to be thrilled. Should I tell him, or do you want to?"

"Why don't we tell him together? Tomorrow after class?"

"Perfect."

They stood together in the parking lot, reluctant to end the evening despite having no particular reason to linger. The easy camaraderie of the video shoot had left them both feeling playful and connected.

"I should get home," Naomi said eventually. "Omari has a book report due tomorrow, and I promised to help him edit it."

"What's the book?"

"One of those graphic novels about weather phenomena. His teacher is letting him use it for the assignment since it got him excited about reading again."

"That's wonderful. What's the report about?"

"How thunderstorms form, but he's written it like a story with characters and dialogue. It's actually pretty creative."

"I'd love to read it sometime, if he's willing to share."

"I'll ask him. He's proud of it, so I think he'd like to show it off."

She moved toward her car, then turned back. "Khadir?"

"Yes?"

"Thank you for being willing to make that silly video. I know it wasn't exactly your thing."

"Actually, it was exactly my thing. I just didn't know it until today."

"What do you mean?"

"Being part of this community, supporting local causes, making a seven-year-old happy—turns out that's very much my thing. Especially when I get to do it with you."

The sincerity in his voice made her breath catch. She stepped closer, rising on her toes to kiss him goodnight. This kiss was soft and sweet, flavored with laughter and shared silliness and the comfortable intimacy that came from two people who genuinely enjoyed each other's company.

"Sweet dreams," she whispered against his lips.

"You too."

As she drove home, Naomi found herself humming the instrumental track from the video shoot. In her rearview mirror, she could see Khadir still standing by his car, watching her drive away with what looked like a smile on his face.

Her phone buzzed at the first red light:

Thank you for being my dance partner tonight. Even if it was just swaying. - K

She typed back:

My pleasure. I haven't giggled that much in years.

Good. You should giggle more often.

Is that a professional recommendation, Mr. Grant?

Personal observation, Ms. Ellis.

I'll take it under advisement. See you Saturday.

Looking forward to it.

At home, Omari was indeed working on his book report, surrounded by colored pencils and index cards covered with notes about cumulonimbus clouds and electrical charges.

"How was class?" he asked without looking up from his drawing of a lightning bolt.

"Good. We learned about gentle exits."

"What's that?"

"Ways to get away from someone who's bothering you without having to hurt them or make a big scene."

"Like what I did with the pencil thing?"

"Exactly like what you did with the pencil thing."

He nodded thoughtfully. "Mr. Khadir says the best victories are the ones where nobody has to lose."

"Mr. Khadir is very wise."

"Are you and Mr. Khadir going to get married?"

The question, delivered with the same casual tone he'd used to ask about gentle exits, made Naomi choke on her sip of water.

"What makes you ask that?"

"You smile different when you talk about him. And you've been humming a lot lately. Plus, Mrs. Patterson told Mrs. Williams that you two looked 'serious' at the ice cream place."

The small-town gossip network never failed to amaze her. "Mrs. Patterson needs to mind her own business."

"So are you?"

"Omari, we're still figuring out what we are to each other. But I promise, if anything important changes, you'll be the first to know."

"Okay. But for what it's worth, I think he'd be good at being a stepdad. He listens to people, and he's patient, and he makes you laugh the real way instead of the polite way."

The observation was so perceptive it took her breath away. "You pay attention to a lot of things, don't you?"

"I learned to. It used to be important to know what kind of mood Dad was in before I said anything." He looked up from his drawing. "But with Mr. Khadir, I don't have to check first. He's the same nice every time."

The casual reference to walking on eggshells around Andre broke her heart, but the contrast he'd drawn filled her with hope. Consistency, patience, genuine kindness—these were the qualities Omari was learning to expect from the men in his life.

"You know what?" she said, settling into the chair beside him. "I think you're right about Mr. Khadir being good at listening. Want to practice your book report on me? I'd love to hear about how thunderstorms form."

As her son launched into his enthusiastic explanation of atmospheric pressure and electrical charges, Naomi felt a deep sense of contentment settle over her. This was what normal felt like—homework help and gentle teasing, community videos and comfortable conversations, the gradual building of trust and affection with someone who treated both her and her son with consistent respect.

Some exits were dramatic and painful. But the best ones, she was learning, were gentle transitions into something better.

CHAPTER THIRTEEN

Saturday afternoon stretched golden and warm, unseasonably pleasant for late October. Naomi packed sandwiches and fruit while Omari gathered his overnight bag for his sleepover at Mia's house with Tyler—a tradition that had developed over the past month and gave both boys something to look forward to each weekend.

"Are you sure you have everything?" she asked, checking his bag one more time.

"Mom, it's Tyler's house. If I forgot something, Aunt Mia will have it." He slung the bag over his shoulder with the confidence of a child who'd done this routine many times. "Are you and Mr. Khadir going on a date?"

"We're going to have a picnic by the lake," she said carefully. "Why?"

"Because you packed the good sandwiches. The ones with the fancy bread and real turkey instead of the lunch meat." He grinned. "Plus you're wearing the pretty earrings again."

She touched her earlobes self-consciously. She had indeed chosen the silver ones her grandmother had given her.

"Enjoy your sleepover," she said, deflecting. "And remember to thank Mia for having you."

"I always do. Have fun on your not-date date."

After dropping Omari at Mia's, Naomi drove to the lake trail parking area where she'd agreed to meet Khadir. She found him loading a blanket and cooler into a backpack, dressed in jeans and a soft gray henley that made him look relaxed and approachable.

"Perfect timing," he said, looking up as she approached. "I was just wondering if I'd packed too much food."

"What did you bring?"

"Mrs. Zhang insisted on sending lo mein and spring rolls. Said picnics needed more than just sandwiches." He hefted the pack onto his shoulders. "I think she's determined to feed half the town through me."

"She's probably succeeding. I brought sandwiches and fruit, so between us we should be well covered."

They set off along the lake trail, walking easily together as they had that afternoon when he'd posted his first event flyer. The path was moderately busy with other weekend visitors, but they found a secluded spot on the far side of the lake where the trail curved away from the main walking area.

Khadir spread the blanket on a patch of soft grass overlooking the water while Naomi unpacked their food. The view was peaceful—late afternoon light dancing on the lake's surface, a few ducks paddling near the shore, the distant sound of children playing at the main beach area.

"This is perfect," she said, settling onto the blanket. "I can't remember the last time I just sat by water and enjoyed the quiet."

"It's one of my favorite spots. I come here sometimes when I need to think through problems or just decompress after difficult days."

They ate and talked, the conversation flowing as easily as it always did between them. Khadir asked about her work, and she found herself describing the satisfaction of matching reluctant readers with books that sparked their interest. He told her about his students' progress, about the community connections the dojo was fostering, about his hopes for expanding the youth scholarship program.

"You know," Naomi said, lying back on the blanket and looking up at the sky, "I never thought I'd be the kind of person who could just... exist peacefully like this. Without planning the next thing or worrying about potential problems."

"What changed?"

She considered the question, watching clouds drift overhead. "I learned the difference between being careful and being afraid. For years, I thought hypervigilance was just good planning. Always anticipating Andre's moods, always trying to prevent conflicts before they started, always having backup plans for my backup plans."

"And now?"

"Now I'm learning to tell the difference between actual problems that need solving and imaginary problems that anxiety creates." She turned to look at him. "The jiu-jitsu helped with that. Learning to read real threats versus perceived ones."

Khadir stretched out beside her, close enough that she could feel the warmth of his arm near hers. "Anxiety lies to us sometimes. Makes everything feel urgent and dangerous when it's not."

"Exactly. Andre used to say I was 'too sensitive' or 'too reactive,' but really I was just trying to survive in a situation that actually was unstable and unpredictable." She paused. "It's taken me a while to trust that not all environments are like that."

"This environment isn't like that," he said quietly.

"No. It's not." She turned onto her side to face him fully. "You're not like that."

They lay looking at each other in the late afternoon light,

and Naomi felt something shift between them. Not dramatically, but like a door opening quietly, revealing a room she'd been afraid to enter.

"Can I tell you something?" she asked.

"Always."

"I used to think love was supposed to be difficult. Like if it wasn't painful or complicated, it wasn't real." She reached out to trace a pattern on the blanket between them. "Andre convinced me that his jealousy meant he loved me deeply, that his need to control my schedule was protective, that his criticism was just honesty."

Khadir's jaw tightened slightly, but he didn't interrupt.

"Being with you is teaching me that love can be steady instead of dramatic. That someone can care about me without needing to manage me." She met his eyes. "It's terrifying and wonderful at the same time."

"Why terrifying?"

"Because it means I might have spent years accepting much less than I deserved. Because it means I have to recalibrate everything I thought I knew about relationships." She paused. "Because it means letting myself hope for something I'm not sure I know how to maintain."

"Naomi." He reached out to cover her hand with his. "You don't have to know how to maintain anything except being yourself. The rest we figure out as we go."

"Is that how it works? Just being ourselves and seeing what happens?"

"That's how the good ones work."

The conviction in his voice made something loosen in her chest. For months, she'd been trying to anticipate what he might want from her, how she should behave to keep his interest, what version of herself might be worthy of his patience and kindness. The idea that she could simply be herself—flawed, learning, sometimes anxious—and that might be enough felt revolutionary.

"What about you?" she asked. "What are you learning?"

He was quiet for a long moment, his thumb tracing gentle patterns across her knuckles.

"I'm learning that some things are worth waiting for," he said finally. "That patience isn't the same as passivity. That caring about someone doesn't mean trying to fix their problems for them."

"That last one must be difficult for you. You're naturally protective."

"It is difficult. There are times I want to solve things for you, especially with your ex-husband. But I'm learning that supporting someone is different from rescuing them."

She studied his face, noting the way afternoon light caught the gold flecks in his brown eyes, the careful way he chose his words when talking about difficult subjects.

"Khadir?"

"Yes?"

"I'm glad we found each other again. Even if it took seventeen years."

"Especially because it took seventeen years," he said. "We're both different people now than we were then. Better people, I think."

"How so?"

"I was so worried about being worthy of good things at seventeen. Spent so much energy trying to prove myself instead of just living authentically." He shifted closer. "You were carrying the weight of everyone else's expectations. Trying to be perfect instead of just being yourself."

"And now?"

"Now I know worthiness isn't something you earn. And you know your own value isn't determined by other people's approval."

The observation was so accurate it made her breath catch. "When did you get so wise?"

"Somewhere between learning to fall safely and learning to get back up on purpose."

She laughed, recognizing her own words from that first day at the dojo. "That's a very martial arts answer."

"It's a very life answer."

The sun was beginning to sink lower, painting the lake in shades of gold and amber. Other picnickers were packing up and heading home, leaving them in increasing privacy as the afternoon wound toward evening.

"I should probably think about heading home soon," Naomi said, though she made no move to sit up.

"Probably," Khadir agreed, also not moving.

They lay there as the shadows lengthened, talking quietly about small things—Omari's upcoming stripe test, the dojo's holiday schedule, books Naomi was ordering for the library's winter reading program. Normal conversation that felt intimate simply because of their proximity, the setting, the knowledge that they had chosen to spend this time together.

"Naomi," Khadir said eventually.

"Mm?"

"Would you like to have dinner at my place? Nothing fancy— I could cook something simple, we could continue talking somewhere more private."

The invitation hung between them, loaded with possibility and the promise of deeper intimacy. Naomi felt her heart rate quicken, not with anxiety but with anticipation.

"I'd like that," she said. "I'd like that very much."

They packed up their picnic slowly, reluctant to end the peaceful interlude by the lake. As they walked back along the trail, Naomi felt a sense of anticipation building—not nervous energy, but the quiet excitement of knowing she was moving toward something good.

Khadir's house was a small craftsman bungalow on Maple Street, painted sage green with white trim and a front porch that invited lingering. Inside, it was exactly what she'd expected—clean and comfortable, with warm colors and careful details that spoke of someone who'd created a genuine home rather than just a place to sleep.

"This is lovely," she said, taking in the built-in bookshelves, the comfortable furniture, the photographs that revealed glimpses of his family and military service.

"Thank you. I've been working on it gradually—refinishing floors, updating the kitchen, making it mine."

He moved around the kitchen with easy competence, pulling ingredients from the refrigerator and starting water for pasta. Naomi settled at the kitchen island, content to watch him work and continue their conversation.

"Can I help with anything?"

"Just keep me company. This is simple enough—pasta with vegetables and a good sauce. Nothing too ambitious."

As he cooked, they talked about everything and nothing. Naomi felt herself relaxing completely, the last vestiges of her usual wariness dissolving in the warmth of his kitchen, the comfort of his presence, the knowledge that she was exactly where she wanted to be.

They ate dinner at his small table, candles flickering between them as full darkness settled outside. The food was delicious, but more than that, the evening felt significant—a claiming of space and time for just the two of them, away from the dojo and community events and all the contexts where they usually saw each other.

"Thank you," Naomi said as they finished eating. "This was perfect. The picnic, dinner, all of it."

"Thank you for saying yes. For trusting me with your afternoon."

They moved to the living room, settling on his couch with

glasses of wine and the comfortable intimacy that had been building all day. When Khadir reached for her, drawing her closer until she was curled against his side, it felt like the most natural thing in the world.

"Naomi," he said softly.

She looked up to find him studying her face with an expression she recognized—want mixed with patience, desire tempered by respect.

"Yes?"

"I care about you. More than I think I've ever cared about anyone."

The words sent warmth flooding through her chest. "I care about you too."

"And I want you to know—whatever happens tonight, whatever doesn't happen, it doesn't change anything between us. There's no pressure, no expectations."

She reached up to cup his face, feeling the slight roughness of his evening beard under her palm. "What if I want something to happen?"

"Then we'll take it as slowly as you need."

She kissed him then, soft at first and then with growing certainty as he responded. This felt right—not rushed or desperate, but inevitable. The natural progression of all the careful trust-building, all the patient getting to know each other, all the moments of choosing each other again and again.

When they finally broke apart, breathless and warm, she looked into his eyes and saw everything she'd been hoping to find—respect, desire, genuine affection, and the promise of a man who would never ask her to be anything other than exactly who she was.

"Stay," he whispered against her forehead.

"Yes," she whispered back. "I'd like to stay."

CHAPTER FOURTEEN

"Stay," he whispered against her forehead.

"Yes," she whispered back. "I'd like to stay."

Khadir pulled back to look at her, searching her face in the soft lamplight. "Are you sure?"

"I'm sure." Her voice was steady, certain. "I've never been more sure of anything."

He cupped her face in his hands, thumbs tracing the line of her cheekbones. "We can take this as slowly as you want."

"I know. That's part of what makes this feel right." She leaned into his touch. "You've never made me feel like I had to be anything other than myself."

He kissed her then, soft and deliberate, pouring months of patient affection into the connection of their lips. When they broke apart, she was smiling—not the careful, composed smile she wore in public, but something warm and unguarded that made his heart race.

"Come on," she said, taking his hand. "Show me the rest of your house."

His bedroom was simple—clean lines, warm colors, a large window that faced the back garden. She moved around the space with gentle curiosity, noting the photographs on his dresser, the books on his nightstand, the way everything was organized but lived-in.

"It feels like you," she said, turning to face him. "Steady and comfortable and safe."

"Is that what I feel like to you?"

"Among other things." She stepped closer, her hands coming up to rest on his chest. "You feel like home, Khadir. Like the person I've been looking for without knowing I was searching."

The words hit him with unexpected force. "Naomi—"

"I love you," she said simply. "I know it's soon to say it out loud, but I love you. The way you listen, the way you see people, the way you've been so patient with both Omari and me. I love the life you've built and the man you've become and the way you make me feel like the best version of myself."

"I love you too," he said, the words flowing easily after months of feeling them without speaking them. "I've been in love with you since high school, and falling in love with the woman you are now has been the greatest privilege of my life."

She rose on her toes to kiss him, and this time the kiss carried the weight of their declarations. When her hands began working at the buttons of his shirt, he covered them with his own.

"You're sure?" he asked one more time.

"I'm sure. Are you?"

"More sure than I've ever been of anything."

She finished unbuttoning his shirt, her fingers gentle as she pushed the fabric from his shoulders. He shivered slightly at her touch—not from cold, but from the simple wonder of being touched with such care, such intention.

"You're beautiful," she whispered, her hands exploring the planes of his chest, the definition of his shoulders that spoke of years of disciplined training.

"So are you." His voice was rough with emotion as he reached for the hem of her sweater. "May I?"

She nodded, lifting her arms to let him pull the soft fabric over her head. For a moment they simply looked at each other in the lamplight, taking in this new level of vulnerability, this crossing of a threshold they'd been approaching with such careful steps.

"I want to memorize this," she said softly. "The way you're looking at me right now. Like I'm something precious."

"You are something precious. You're everything."

When he lifted her, she wrapped her arms around his neck, pressing her forehead to his as he carried her the few steps to his bed. He set her down gently, his hands framing her face as he looked into her eyes one more time.

"I love you," she whispered.

"I love you too," he whispered back, and as she drew him down to her, the rest of the world faded away.

KHADIR WOKE BEFORE DAWN, as he had every morning for the past fifteen years. Military habits died hard, even when there was no longer any practical need for pre-sunrise alertness. But this morning felt different—weighted with significance and touched with a contentment he hadn't experienced in years.

Naomi lay curled against his side, her natural curls spread across the pillow they'd somehow ended up sharing, her breathing deep and even in sleep. In the pale light filtering through his bedroom curtains, she looked peaceful in a way he'd never seen before. Not the careful composure she wore in public, not the gentle vigilance she maintained even during their most relaxed conversations, but true rest.

He let himself study her face in the quiet morning light—the curve of her cheekbone, the soft fullness of her lips, the way her eyelashes cast tiny shadows on her skin. She was beautiful, but more than that, she was here. In his bed, in his arms, trusting him with her vulnerability in a way that made his chest tight with gratitude and fierce protectiveness.

She stirred slightly, her hand moving across his chest in sleep, and he covered it with his own. This was what he'd been waiting for without fully realizing it—not just physical intimacy, but this sense of rightness, of two lives beginning to interweave in ways both profound and wonderfully ordinary.

"Good morning," she murmured, her eyes fluttering open to find him watching her.

"Good morning. Did you sleep well?"

"Better than I have in months." She stretched slightly, then settled more fully against his side. "What time is it?"

"Early. Six-thirty, maybe. The sun's just coming up."

"Mmm. I don't have to pick up Omari until noon." She pressed a kiss to his collarbone, right over the scar she'd traced so gently the night before. "Do we have to get up right now?"

"Not if you don't want to."

"I don't want to. I want to stay right here and pretend the rest of the world doesn't exist for a few more hours."

"I can work with that plan."

They lay together in comfortable silence, watching the morning light grow stronger through his bedroom window. Eventually, the practical needs of Sunday morning began to assert themselves—coffee, breakfast, the gentle transition back to the ordinary world that waited beyond his front door.

"I could make us breakfast," Khadir offered. "Nothing fancy, but I make decent pancakes."

"I'd love that. But first..." She propped herself up on one elbow to look at him properly. "Last night was beautiful. I want you to know that. I feel... different. In the best possible way."

"Different how?"

"Like I remember what it feels like to be genuinely happy.

Not just content or getting by, but actually happy." She leaned down to kiss him, slow and sweet. "Thank you for being so patient with me. For waiting until I was ready."

"Thank you for trusting me with this. With you."

They made breakfast together in his kitchen, moving around each other with an easy intimacy that felt both new and natural. Naomi wore one of his t-shirts, which fell to mid-thigh and made her look younger and more relaxed than he'd ever seen her. He found himself stealing glances as she set the table, noting the way she hummed under her breath, the comfortable way she'd claimed space in his home.

"This feels remarkably normal," she observed as they sat down with coffee and pancakes. "I was worried it might be awkward this morning."

"Why would it be awkward?"

"I don't know. It's been so long since I've done this—woken up in someone else's bed, had morning-after conversation." She took a sip of coffee. "With Andre, intimate moments were always followed by... analysis. Discussion of how I'd performed, what could be improved, whether I'd been sufficiently appreciative."

Khadir's jaw tightened at the casual way she described such an awful violation of intimacy. "That's not how this works."

"I know that now. But old habits die hard, you know? Part of me was preparing for a critique session."

"The only thing I want to say about last night is that I love you, and I feel incredibly lucky that you chose to share that with me."

Her smile was radiant. "See? That's exactly what I mean about you being different. Better."

After breakfast, they worked together to clean up—washing dishes, wiping down counters, the kind of domestic teamwork that spoke of compatibility in small, important ways. When

Naomi's phone chimed with a text from Mia, reality began to reassert itself.

Boys are having a great time. Pickup still good for noon? - M

"I should probably head home in an hour or so," Naomi said, showing him the message. "Shower, change clothes, try to look like I didn't spend the night elsewhere before I collect my son."

"Of course. Though for what it's worth, you look perfect exactly as you are."

"In your t-shirt and yesterday's jeans? I think the mothers at Mia's house might have questions."

"Let them have questions."

She laughed. "Easy for you to say. You don't have to navigate small-town gossip as a single mother who's trying to maintain her reputation."

The comment reminded him of the reality they'd be returning to—the careful balance she maintained between her own happiness and her responsibility to Omari, the way their relationship would be observed and discussed and potentially judged by others.

"Are you worried about that? About what people will say?"

She considered the question while finishing her coffee. "Not worried, exactly. But aware. Omari's at an age where he notices things, asks questions. I want to be thoughtful about how we handle this."

"What does thoughtful look like to you?"

"Honest but age-appropriate. Steady rather than dramatic. I want him to see that relationships can be healthy and support-ive, but I don't want to overwhelm him with changes too quickly."

Khadir nodded, understanding the delicate balance she was trying to maintain. "We go at whatever pace feels right for both of you."

"Thank you for understanding that. Andre always pushed for more, faster—more time together, more public displays, more integration into Omari's life. It felt like he was trying to establish ownership rather than build genuine connection."

"This isn't ownership, Naomi. This is partnership."

"I know. That's what makes it so different. So much better."

As she got ready to leave, Khadir found himself reluctant to end the intimacy of the morning. Not the physical intimacy—though he'd certainly miss having her in his arms—but the emotional closeness, the sense of being part of a team, the glimpse of what their future might look like if they continued building it together.

"Same time Tuesday for class?" he asked as she gathered her things.

"Definitely. Though I might need to work extra hard to concentrate on hip escapes instead of remembering last night."

"I might have the same problem."

At his front door, she rose on her toes to kiss him goodbye. This kiss was different from all the others they'd shared—deeper, more certain, flavored with the knowledge of what they now meant to each other.

"I love you," she said against his lips.

"I love you too. Drive safcly."

"See you Tuesday."

As he watched her car disappear around the corner, Khadir felt a profound sense of contentment settle over him. The careful patience of the past months had led to this—not just a night of physical intimacy, but the beginning of something that felt permanent, significant, worth every moment of waiting.

His phone buzzed with a text:

Thank you for the most beautiful night and the most perfect morning. I love you. - N

He typed back:

> Thank you for trusting me with your heart. I love you too. Always.

> Always.

Walking back into his house, Khadir could still smell her perfume on his shirt, could still see the impression her head had left on his pillow. The ordinary spaces of his home had been transformed by her presence, and he found himself hoping it was the first of many such transformations.

Some mornings changed everything. This, he knew with absolute certainty, had been one of those mornings.

CHAPTER FIFTEEN

The post appeared on the Sweetgum Community Facebook page Tuesday morning at 7:43 AM, just as Naomi was finishing her coffee and getting ready to leave for work.

Just wondering if anyone else thinks it's appropriate for teachers to be dating their students' instructors? Seems like a conflict of interest to me. What happens to professional boundaries when personal relationships get involved?

The post had no name attached—just one of those anonymous community accounts that people used when they wanted to stir up drama without taking responsibility for it. But the timing, coming just two days after her night with Khadir, felt deliberate and pointed.

Mia texted her the screenshot at 8:15:

Seen this? Don't let it get to you. Anonymous keyboard warriors aren't worth your energy.

By lunch, three people had forwarded her the post. By

dismissal, it had thirty-seven comments, ranging from supportive ("Mind your own business—Naomi Ellis is a wonderful person") to judgmental ("Teachers should set better examples") to practical ("As long as the child isn't getting special treatment, what's the problem?").

Naomi sat in her car in the school parking lot, staring at her phone screen and feeling sick to her stomach. She'd known this might happen eventually—small towns thrived on gossip, and her relationship with Khadir had been increasingly visible over the past month. But seeing it laid out so starkly, framed as something potentially inappropriate or unprofessional, made her want to disappear.

Her phone rang. Khadir's name appeared on the screen.

"Hi," she said, her voice smaller than she intended.

"I saw the post," he said without preamble. "Are you okay?"

"I don't know. Maybe. I knew people were talking, but seeing it written out like that..." She trailed off, watching other teachers walk to their cars with normal Tuesday concerns—lesson planning, grocery lists, carpools to manage.

"Do you want to talk about it? In person, I mean?"

"I should get home. Omari will be wondering where I am."

"Of course. But Naomi? This doesn't change anything for me. Not the post, not whatever people are saying, nothing."

"It might change things for Omari. For my job. For—" She stopped herself before listing all the catastrophic possibilities her anxiety was generating.

"Hey. Breathe. We'll figure this out together, okay? One step at a time."

His voice was steady, calm, exactly what she needed to hear. But even so, the drive home felt endless, her mind cycling through worst-case scenarios and damage control strategies.

❦

OMARI WAS at the kitchen table when she walked in, homework spread around him in his usual organized chaos. He looked up with a smile that immediately shifted to concern when he saw her face.

"What's wrong?" he asked.

She set her purse down carefully, buying time to figure out how much to explain. "Someone posted something online about me and Mr. Khadir. Something not very nice."

"What kind of something?"

"They think it might be inappropriate for us to date since I work at your school and he's your instructor."

Omari considered this with the serious expression he wore when processing complex information. "But that's stupid. You're not my teacher, and he doesn't give me grades. Plus, you're both grown-ups."

The simple logic of his response made her smile despite everything. "You're right, it is stupid. But sometimes people like to have opinions about other people's lives."

"Like Dad does."

The observation was matter-of-fact, but it hit like a physical blow. "What do you mean?"

"He always has opinions about what you should do, who you should be friends with, how you should act. Even though you're divorced and he doesn't live here anymore." Omari looked back down at his math worksheet. "I think he might be the one who posted that thing."

Naomi's blood ran cold. "What makes you say that?"

"Because he asked me weird questions last weekend. About Mr. Khadir, about whether you two go places together, about whether Mr. Khadir comes to our house." He erased something on his paper with more force than necessary. "I told him it wasn't his business."

Pride and anxiety warred in her chest. Pride that her son had stood up for their privacy, anxiety about Andre's response to being told off by a ten-year-old.

"What did he say when you told him that?"

"He said everything about my life is his business because he's my dad. But I don't think that's true. I think some things are just ours."

The wisdom in his words made her throat tight. "You're absolutely right. Some things are just ours."

Her phone buzzed with a text from an unknown number:

> Saw the Facebook post. We need to discuss how your personal choices are affecting our son.

She took a screenshot and added it to her documentation folder without responding. Whatever Andre's involvement in the anonymous post, engaging with his manufactured outrage would only make things worse.

"Mom?" Omari was watching her with those perceptive eyes that missed nothing. "Are you going to stop seeing Mr. Khadir because people are being mean?"

The question cut straight to the heart of her fear. "Do you think I should?"

"No. I think you should do what makes you happy, and Mr. Khadir makes you happy." He paused. "Plus, if you stop doing things every time someone complains, you'll never get to do anything good."

WEDNESDAY EVENING'S class felt different from the moment Naomi walked into the dojo. The usual warm atmosphere was still there, but she found herself hyperaware of every interaction, every glance, every moment when other parents might be watching her and Khadir together.

"Focus on your breathing," Khadir said during warm-ups, and she realized she'd been holding her breath without realizing it.

The techniques came harder tonight—her hip escapes were tentative, her technical stand-ups lacked their usual confidence. She felt like she was performing rather than learning, conscious of being observed in a way that made everything feel artificial.

"Can we talk after class?" Khadir asked quietly during a water break.

She nodded, not trusting her voice.

After the other students left, she found herself alone with Khadir and Kiana in the quiet dojo. Omari was helping Kiana organize equipment, giving them a few minutes of relative privacy.

"How are you holding up?" Khadir asked.

"I keep thinking I should step back," she said without preamble. "From the classes, from... us. Until things die down."

Khadir was quiet for a long moment. "Is that what you want to do?"

"I don't know what I want to do. I just know I don't want my personal life to become a problem for Omari, or for your business, or for my job."

"What if we made some adjustments instead of stepping back completely?"

"What kind of adjustments?"

Kiana approached before he could answer, having apparently finished organizing with Omari's help.

"Sorry to interrupt," she said, "but I couldn't help overhearing. I have some thoughts, if you want to hear them."

Naomi looked between them, noting the way they seemed to communicate without words—the kind of professional partnership built on trust and shared values.

"Please," she said.

"First," Kiana said, settling into one of the chairs near the front desk, "whoever posted that anonymous garbage can take a long walk off a short pier. You've done nothing wrong, and anyone with eyes can see that you and Khadir treat each other and Omari with nothing but respect."

"But?" Naomi could hear the qualifying word coming.

"But we could make some small changes that address any legitimate concerns while keeping you both in training and in each other's lives." Kiana looked to Khadir. "Group classes only when you're both here. No private lessons. Other instructors or parents present during any conversations about Omari's progress."

"Basically, glass house policies," Khadir added. "Nothing to hide, everything visible."

Naomi considered this. "You'd be willing to do that? Change how you run your business because of gossip?"

"I'd be willing to do that because I care about you and Omari, and I want you both to feel comfortable here," Khadir said. "The dojo's mission is creating safe spaces for learning and growth. If adjusting some procedures helps you feel safer, then that's what we'll do."

"What about us? Our relationship?"

"What about it?" Khadir's voice was steady, certain. "We're two adults who care about each other. We're not doing anything inappropriate, we're not violating any actual policies, and we're not hurting anyone. If people want to manufacture drama where none exists, that's their choice. It doesn't have to be ours."

Kiana nodded. "Plus, half the people commenting probably don't even know you personally. Anonymous internet outrage isn't the same as real community concern."

Omari appeared beside them, having apparently been listening from the equipment area. "Are you talking about the mean Facebook post?"

"How did you—" Naomi started.

"Tyler's mom told him about it. He asked me if you and Mr.

Khadir were in trouble." Omari looked between the adults with his usual directness. "I told him no, because you're not doing anything wrong. You're just happy."

The simple statement hit with more force than any complex argument. *You're just happy.*

"You know what?" Naomi said, feeling something settle in her chest. "You're absolutely right. I am happy. We're not doing anything wrong, and I'm not going to let anonymous internet trolls take that away from us."

"So you'll keep coming to classes?" Khadir asked.

"I'll keep coming to classes. With the boundary adjustments Kiana suggested, because they make sense regardless of gossip." She looked around the dojo—the place where she'd learned to fall safely, to stand up with purpose, to trust her instincts and create space when she needed it. "This is my place too now. I'm not giving it up because someone else has a problem with my choices."

"Good," Kiana said with satisfaction. "Because you're one of our best students, and we'd hate to lose you to manufactured drama."

"Plus," Omari added pragmatically, "you haven't earned your first stripe yet. You can't quit before you get your stripe."

The comment made all three adults laugh, breaking the tension that had been building since the anonymous post appeared.

"He's right," Khadir said. "Can't quit before the stripe. That's probably an actual rule."

As they gathered their things to leave, Naomi felt lighter than she had all week. The post was still there, the comments were still circulating, and Andre was probably still manufacturing outrage. But none of that changed the fundamental truth: she was building something good with someone who respected her, in a community that was learning to support both her and her son.

"Thank you," she said to Khadir as they walked to their cars. "For the boundary suggestions, for being willing to adjust things, for not making me feel like my concerns were silly."

"Your concerns aren't silly. Protecting what matters to you is never silly."

"What matters to me is this," she said, gesturing between them. "You, Omari, the life we're building together. I'm not letting anonymous cowards take that away."

"Good," he said, and leaned down to kiss her forehead. "Because I'm not going anywhere."

Driving home, Naomi felt a familiar sense of strength settling into her bones. The same feeling she got after a good class at the dojo—centered, capable, ready to handle whatever came next. Some battles were worth fighting, and some things were worth protecting.

This was both.

CHAPTER SIXTEEN

The text from Andre came at 6:23 AM on Thursday, just as Khadir was finishing his morning coffee and reviewing his schedule for the day.

> Need to discuss the inappropriate relationship between my son's martial arts instructor and his mother. This affects my parental rights.

Khadir read the message twice, noting the careful language designed to sound legal and threatening. He'd expected something like this ever since the anonymous Facebook post, but seeing Andre's name attached to the harassment felt different—more personal, more calculated.

He forwarded the message to Naomi with a simple note:

> FYI. Don't respond to him directly.

Her reply came within minutes:

Already got three messages from him this morning. Screenshotting everything for documentation. Sorry he's dragging you into his drama.

You don't need to apologize for his behavior. We knew this might happen.

I know. Still sorry. See you tonight for class.

Looking forward to it.

But as Khadir went through his morning routine—reviewing lesson plans, checking equipment, responding to emails from potential new students—Andre's message lingered in the back of his mind like a persistent ache. Not because he was worried about the man's empty legal threats, but because he recognized the pattern. This was how bullies escalated when their initial attempts at control failed.

At 9 AM, Kiana arrived with coffee and a grim expression.

"Heard about the text messages," she said without preamble. "Mrs. Zhang mentioned that Andre Pierce was in the restaurant last night, making loud comments about 'protecting his son from inappropriate influences.'"

"Of course he was." Khadir accepted the coffee gratefully. "How public was this performance?"

"Public enough. Mrs. Zhang said he seemed to be playing to an audience, making sure other customers could hear his concerns about 'professional boundaries' and 'what's best for the child.'"

Khadir felt his jaw tighten. Andre wasn't just harassing Naomi directly—he was trying to build a narrative in the community, positioning himself as the concerned father protecting his son from some imaginary threat.

"What's our policy on this?" he asked.

"Legally? He can't do anything to us. We're not violating any actual regulations, and there's no law against adults dating each other." Kiana settled behind the front desk, pulling out her laptop. "Practically? We stick to the glass house policies we discussed. Everything visible, everything documented, no private interactions between you and Naomi regarding Omari."

"And if he keeps escalating?"

"Then we document everything and let him dig his own grave. Bullies usually overplay their hand eventually."

The morning classes went smoothly—a group of home-schooled teenagers working on advanced techniques, followed by the senior citizens class that had started coming after the Confidence & Kindness Night. But Khadir found himself checking his phone more frequently than usual, half-expecting another message from Andre or news that the situation had somehow gotten worse.

At lunch, he drove to Sweet and Spicy Chinese Palace for takeout, partly because he was craving Mrs. Zhang's spring rolls and partly because he wanted to gauge the community temperature firsthand.

"Khadir!" Mrs. Zhang greeted him with her usual warmth, but he caught the slight tension around her eyes. "The usual?"

"Please. And Mrs. Zhang? I heard Andre Pierce was here last night."

Her expression darkened. "That man has no shame. Making a spectacle of himself, trying to get other customers to agree with his complaints about you and Naomi." She shook her head. "Most people just looked uncomfortable and changed the subject."

"Most people?"

"Mrs. Crenshaw seemed interested in his concerns. But that woman loves drama more than she loves her own grandchildren." Mrs. Zhang leaned across the counter conspiratorially.

"Everyone else thinks he's just a bitter ex-husband trying to cause trouble."

"That's what I was hoping."

"You and Naomi are good people. That little boy is lucky to have both of you in his life." She handed him his order with a firm nod. "Don't let one bitter man make you doubt that."

The afternoon brought two new student inquiries—both families who'd heard about the dojo through word-of-mouth recommendations from current students. Khadir found himself paying extra attention to their questions, noting how they asked about class structure, safety protocols, and instructor qualifications. Normal concerns from parents considering martial arts for their children, not the loaded questions he might expect if Andre's campaign was gaining traction.

By 4 PM, he felt cautiously optimistic that whatever damage Andre was trying to inflict wasn't spreading beyond his own bitter circle.

Then Naomi arrived for evening class, and he could see the strain in the careful way she held her shoulders, the practiced smile that didn't quite reach her eyes.

"Long day?" he asked as she signed Omari in for class.

"Three more text messages, two voicemails, and a call to the school secretary asking about 'policies regarding staff members' personal relationships.'" She kept her voice low, aware of other parents within earshot. "Mrs. Henderson told him that staff personal lives weren't school business unless they impacted job performance, which apparently wasn't the answer he wanted."

"What did he say to that?"

"According to Mrs. Henderson, he started talking about 'protecting his parental rights' and 'ensuring appropriate role models for his child.' She hung up on him."

Khadir felt a surge of gratitude for the school secretary's no-nonsense approach. "Good for her."

"The problem is, he's not wrong about having parental

rights. If he decides to make Omari's training an issue in their custody arrangement..." She trailed off, but he could see the worry in her eyes.

"Has he done that before? Used custody threats to control your decisions?"

"It's his favorite weapon. Anytime I do something he doesn't approve of, he threatens to take me back to court for modification of custody or visitation." She glanced over at Omari, who was warming up with the other kids, completely absorbed in his pre-class routine. "Usually it's empty threats, but the legal fees alone..."

Khadir understood. Andre didn't need to win in court—he just needed to make fighting expensive and exhausting enough that Naomi would capitulate rather than risk her financial stability.

"What can I do to help?"

"Just... be patient with all this. With the extra boundaries, with me being nervous, with whatever other drama he decides to manufacture." She looked up at him with apologetic eyes. "I know this isn't what you signed up for."

"Naomi." He waited until she met his gaze fully. "I signed up for you. All of you, including the complicated parts. A bitter ex-husband trying to cause trouble doesn't change that."

Some of the tension left her shoulders. "Thank you. For saying that, for meaning it."

"I do mean it."

Class proceeded normally, with Khadir and Kiana maintaining the new protocols they'd established—group instruction only, other adults present during any discussions, everything visible and documented. If the other parents noticed the extra formality, they didn't comment on it.

During a water break, Mr. Peterson from the hardware store approached Khadir.

"Heard there's been some drama on social media," he said

bluntly. "Want you to know I think it's ridiculous. You run a good program here, and what you do in your personal life is nobody's business but yours."

"I appreciate that, Mr. Peterson."

"My grandson's been coming to classes for two months now. Kid was getting picked on at school, had no confidence, wouldn't stand up for himself." The older man gestured toward where his grandson was practicing breakfalls with focused concentration. "Look at him now. Whatever you're doing, it's working."

"That's all him. I just provided some tools."

"Don't sell yourself short. And don't let some bitter trouble-maker make you doubt the good work you're doing."

As Mr. Peterson returned to watching class, Khadir felt the same cautious optimism he'd experienced earlier. The community members who actually knew him, who'd seen the positive impact of his work, weren't buying into Andre's manufactured outrage.

After class, as families began leaving, Andre's custody threat hung unspoken in the air between Khadir and Naomi. They'd maintained professional boundaries throughout the evening, but the careful distance felt artificial and sad.

"Walk you to your car?" Khadir asked, noting that most other families had already left.

"That would be nice."

Outside, the October evening was crisp and clear, full of the promise of changing seasons. Under normal circumstances, it would have been the kind of night that invited lingering, maybe a quick kiss goodnight, certainly the comfortable intimacy they'd been building over the past weeks.

Instead, they maintained careful space between them as they walked.

"I hate this," Naomi said quietly when they reached her car. "I hate that he's making something beautiful feel complicated and fraught."

"It's still beautiful," Khadir said. "He can't change that."

"Can't he? When I'm second-guessing every interaction, when I'm worried about how things look instead of how they feel?"

"That's his goal—to make you doubt yourself, to make you choose anxiety over happiness." Khadir leaned against his own car, maintaining the physical distance while offering emotional closeness. "Don't give him that power."

"Easier said than done."

"I know. But Naomi? Whatever he throws at us next, we handle it together. You don't have to manage his drama alone anymore."

She was quiet for a long moment, keys jingling softly in her hand. "What if he actually follows through on the custody threat? What if he makes this into a legal issue?"

"Then we deal with that too. You've been documenting everything, you have community support, and you're not doing anything wrong." His voice was steady, certain. "Most importantly, Omari knows the truth about what's happening. He's old enough to have opinions about his own life."

"You really think it'll be okay?"

"I think you're stronger than you know, and I think Andre is weaker than he pretends. Bullies usually are."

As she drove away, Khadir stood in the parking lot for a moment, looking up at the stars appearing over Sweetgum. Tomorrow would bring new challenges—more of Andre's manufactured drama, more careful navigation of community politics, more balance between protecting what they'd built and not letting fear control their choices.

But tonight had shown him something important: the people who mattered, the community members who actually knew them, were choosing to see past the gossip and support what was real. Mr. Peterson's grandson practicing his breakfalls with new confidence. Mrs. Zhang defending them to her customers. Mrs. Henderson hanging up on Andre's fishing expedition.

One man's bitterness couldn't destroy what an entire community was choosing to nurture and protect.

His phone buzzed with a text from Naomi:

Thank you for tonight. For being steady when everything else feels shaky. I love you.

He typed back:

I love you too. We've got this.

Yes, we do.

Walking to his car, Khadir felt that familiar sense of resolve settling into his bones. Some lines were worth holding, some ground was worth defending. Whatever Andre threw at them next, they'd meet it together—with patience, documentation, and the quiet strength that came from knowing they were building something worth protecting.

CHAPTER SEVENTEEN

Naomi stayed late Thursday evening to update the library's winter reading display. The halls of Sweetgum Elementary were quiet after hours, filled with the comfortable silence that came with empty classrooms and finished lessons. She'd volunteered for the extra work partly because the display needed attention, and partly because going home to an empty house—Omari was at another sleepover with Tyler—felt less appealing than losing herself in the familiar routine of organizing books and creating inviting spaces for young readers.

She was arranging picture books about snow and winter holidays when she heard footsteps in the hallway outside the library. Not the quick clip of heels that would signal Mrs. Henderson or another staff member, but the heavier stride of someone walking with purpose.

"Naomi."

She looked up to find Andre standing in the library doorway, and her stomach dropped like an elevator with cut cables. He wasn't supposed to be here—visitors were required to check in at the main office, which had been locked for over an hour.

"Andre." She kept her voice level, professional. "The building is closed to visitors. You'll need to come back during regular hours if you need something from the school."

"I need to talk to you about our son." He stepped into the library without invitation, and she noticed he'd positioned himself between her and the door. "About the choices you're making that affect his well-being."

"Our communication goes through the app, as required by our custody agreement." She moved slightly, angling toward the back exit that led to the playground. "If you have concerns about Omari, you can message me there."

"This is too important for text messages." His voice carried that familiar edge—not quite shouting, but loud enough to establish dominance in the quiet space. "This martial arts instructor you're sleeping with—"

"Andre, stop." The words came out sharper than she'd intended, but she didn't soften them. "My personal relationships are not your concern."

"Everything about my son is my concern. And when his mother is making decisions based on her hormones instead of his best interests—"

"I'm going to stop you right there." Naomi set down the book she'd been holding and faced him directly. "Nothing about my relationship with Khadir affects Omari negatively. If anything, he's benefiting from the confidence and skills he's learning."

"Skills?" Andre's voice rose. "You mean violence? You're teaching our son to fight because your boyfriend thinks that's appropriate?"

"I'm teaching our son to protect himself and move through the world with confidence. The same things any good parent would want their child to learn."

"Any good parent would prioritize stability over whatever this is." He gestured dismissively. "Dating your son's instructor, having sleepovers while Omari's conveniently elsewhere—"

The insinuation hit like a slap, and Naomi felt her face flush with anger and embarrassment. "You need to leave. Now."

"I'm not finished."

"Yes, you are." She pulled out her phone. "I'm calling security."

Andre stepped closer, his voice dropping to the intimate, threatening tone she remembered from their marriage. "You always were dramatic. Making everything into a crisis when we could just have a reasonable conversation."

The familiar gaslighting made her stomach clench, but something had shifted in her since those days. Months of martial arts training, weeks of learning to trust her instincts, the knowledge that she had people in her corner who would support her—it all crystallized into clarity.

"This is not a reasonable conversation," she said firmly. "This is harassment. You're in a closed school building without permission, cornering me in my workplace, making inappropriate comments about my personal life. Leave now, or I'm calling the police."

"The police?" He laughed, but there was no humor in it. "Over a conversation between co-parents?"

"Over a man refusing to leave when asked, blocking exits, and creating a hostile environment." She moved toward the back door, keeping her phone visible. "Security will be here in five minutes if you don't go voluntarily."

For a moment, Andre looked like he might escalate further. His jaw tightened, his hands clenched at his sides, and she recognized the body language that had once made her scramble to placate and de-escalate.

But she wasn't that person anymore.

"This isn't over," he said finally.

"Yes, it is. All future communication goes through the app. If you contact me directly again, I'm filing a harassment complaint."

He turned and left without another word, his footsteps echoing down the empty hallway. Naomi waited until she heard the main entrance close, then sank into one of the child-sized chairs, her legs suddenly shaky.

Her hands were trembling as she pulled up Khadir's contact, but she managed to type:

> Andre showed up at school after hours. I handled it, but I'm shaken. Could you come?

His response was immediate:

> On my way. Are you safe?

> Yes. He left. I'm still in the building.

> Stay there. I'll be there in 10 minutes.

She sat in the quiet library, surrounded by books about friendship and courage and characters who faced down monsters both real and imaginary. The familiar space felt different now—not violated exactly, but changed. Andre had brought his toxicity into her sanctuary, and she would need time to reclaim the peace this place usually offered.

Her phone rang. Mrs. Henderson's name appeared on the screen.

"Naomi? I just got an alert that someone used the staff entrance after hours. Is everything okay?"

"It's okay now. Andre came by to... discuss something. He's gone."

"Andre Pierce? Your ex-husband?" Mrs. Henderson's voice sharpened with protective authority. "Honey, he's not authorized to be in this building after hours. I'm filing an incident report."

"Is that necessary? I handled it, and he didn't—"

"He what? Didn't threaten you? Didn't make you feel unsafe? Didn't corner you in your workplace when you couldn't leave?" Mrs. Henderson's tone brooked no argument. "This goes on record, Naomi. You need documentation if this escalates."

"You're right. Thank you."

"Are you still in the building? I can come in—"

"No, I'm fine. Someone's coming to get me."

"Good. And Naomi? You did the right thing by standing up to him. Don't let anyone tell you otherwise."

After she hung up, Naomi sat in the peaceful library and tried to process what had happened. Six months ago, that confrontation would have left her apologizing, questioning herself, wondering what she'd done to provoke Andre's anger.

Tonight, she felt shaken but clear. He had been inappropriate. She had set boundaries. She had protected herself and refused to be drawn into his manipulation. The trembling in her hands wasn't fear—it was adrenaline from standing her ground.

Footsteps in the hallway made her tense, but then she heard Khadir's voice calling her name.

"In here," she called back.

He appeared in the doorway, slightly out of breath, his face tight with concern. When he saw her sitting among the picture books, some of the tension left his shoulders.

"Are you hurt?" he asked, moving toward her but stopping just outside arm's reach—respecting the professional space they maintained at school.

"No. Just shaken." She stood up, grateful for the steadiness of her legs. "He cornered me here, tried to have one of his 'reasonable conversations' about my choices affecting Omari."

"Did he touch you?"

"No. But he positioned himself between me and the exit, used that intimidating voice he perfects—the whole playbook." She picked up her purse and the books she'd been working with.

"I told him to leave, threatened to call security, and he eventually went."

"You handled it perfectly."

"Did I? I keep replaying it, wondering if I should have de-escalated differently—"

"Naomi." His voice was gentle but firm. "You set boundaries, you refused to engage with his manipulation, and you protected yourself. That's exactly what you should have done."

They walked out together, Khadir waiting while she locked the library and then accompanying her to the parking lot. Under the security lights, she could see the careful control in his expression—anger held in check by concern for her wellbeing.

"I want to find him and have a conversation of my own," he said as they reached her car.

"That's exactly what he wants. He's trying to provoke a reaction, create drama he can use to paint himself as the victim."

"I know. Doesn't mean I don't want to do it."

The honesty in his admission made her smile despite the evening's stress. "Your protective instincts are showing, Mr. Grant."

"They tend to do that where you're concerned."

They stood by her car in the quiet parking lot, and Naomi felt the familiar comfort of his presence—steady, supportive, unwavering in his care for her wellbeing.

"I don't want to go home to an empty house tonight," she said quietly. "Would it be okay if I came to your place? Just for company, for feeling safe?"

"Of course. Always."

At Khadir's house, they sat on his couch with cups of tea and talked through the evening's events. Naomi found herself analyzing Andre's tactics, recognizing the patterns she'd once thought were normal relationship dynamics.

"He's escalating because his usual methods aren't working,"

she said. "The anonymous social media posts, the text messages, the public comments at restaurants—none of it is having the effect he wants."

"Which is?"

"Me backing down, ending our relationship, returning to a life where he has more influence over my decisions." She curled up against Khadir's side, grateful for the warmth and steadiness of his presence. "But I'm not the person I was when we were married. I won't be controlled by his tantrums anymore."

"What do you think he'll try next?"

"Probably the custody threat he's been building toward. Frame tonight as evidence that I'm making poor choices that affect Omari, use my 'instability' as grounds for modification." She felt Khadir's arm tighten around her. "But I documented everything, Mrs. Henderson is filing a report, and I have months of evidence showing his escalating behavior."

"And you have a community that sees the truth about who you are and what you're building."

"That too." She tilted her head to look at him. "Thank you for coming tonight. For being exactly who I needed you to be."

"Thank you for calling me. For trusting me with this."

They sat together in comfortable silence, and Naomi felt something settle in her bones that had nothing to do with the evening's confrontation. She had faced down her ex-husband's intimidation tactics and walked away stronger. She had people who supported her, systems in place to protect herself, and the internal confidence to know the difference between actual threats and manufactured drama.

"I love you," she said quietly.

"I love you too."

Outside, the October night was peaceful and clear. Inside, despite everything Andre had tried to disrupt, they were building something real and lasting—something that could weather attempts at sabotage because it was grounded in mutual respect, honest communication, and the kind of love that made both people stronger.

Some confrontations were inevitable. But with the right preparation and the right people in your corner, they could be survived and overcome.

CHAPTER EIGHTEEN

The Sweetgum Fall Heritage Parade happened every year on the second Saturday in November, rain or shine. This year brought crisp sunshine and the kind of blue sky that made the turning leaves look like stained glass windows. Main Street was closed to traffic from Pine to Maple, lined with folding chairs and families claiming their spots with blankets and thermoses of hot coffee.

Khadir stood with his dojo students near the staging area behind Town Hall, helping kids adjust their ghee belts and reminding them about the parade route. The city had invited youth organizations to participate, and fifteen of his students had signed up to march—from six-year-old Sarah Thompson, who kept practicing her bow, to teenage Miguel Rodriguez, who wore his new green belt with obvious pride.

"Remember," he told the group, "we represent more than just ourselves today. We represent the values we train—respect, confidence, community support."

"And good posture," added Kiana, adjusting Omari's collar. "Shoulders back, eyes forward, proud of what you've accomplished."

Down the street, Naomi walked alongside the Sweetgum Elementary reading wagon—a decorated cart pulled by parent volunteers and filled with costumed children holding signs about their favorite books. She wore a bright yellow t-shirt that read "Reading is My Superpower" and carried a stack of bookmarks to hand out to spectators.

Khadir caught sight of her through the crowd and felt the familiar flutter of affection mixed with pride. Three days had passed since Andre's confrontation at the school, and she'd handled the aftermath with remarkable composure—filing reports, documenting incidents, maintaining her professional responsibilities while refusing to let fear dictate her choices.

"There's Ms. Ellis," Omari said, spotting his mother across the staging area. He waved enthusiastically, and she waved back with a smile that reached all the way to where the dojo group was assembled.

"She looks happy," observed Tyler, Mia's nephew who'd joined the dojo two weeks ago.

"She is happy," Omari said with satisfaction. "She smiles the real way now instead of the pretend way."

Khadir caught Kiana's amused glance. In a town the size of Sweetgum, everyone's emotional weather was basically public information, especially when it involved the children's librarian dating the martial arts instructor.

The parade began promptly at ten o'clock with the high school marching band, followed by vintage cars carrying local dignitaries, the volunteer fire department, and various civic organizations. When their turn came, the dojo students fell into formation—older kids in front, younger ones behind, everyone walking with the upright posture and measured pace that came from months of training.

Along the parade route, parents called out encouragement and took pictures. Mrs. Zhang waved from her restaurant's doorway, and Mr. Peterson gave them a thumbs up from his hardware store steps. The community support was visible and vocal, a sharp contrast to the anonymous criticism that had circulated on social media weeks earlier.

As they passed the area where families from Sweetgum Elementary were gathered, Khadir found himself scanning for Naomi. He spotted her distributing bookmarks to children, talking animatedly with parents about upcoming reading programs, fully engaged in her role as community educator and literacy advocate.

Their eyes met across the organized chaos of the parade route. She was too far away for conversation, but her smile was warm and genuine—not the careful, professional expression she might have worn weeks ago when their relationship was still tentative, but the open, affectionate look of someone who was no longer hiding her feelings from her community.

He smiled back, a small acknowledgment that felt significant in its publicness. Here, in front of half the town, they were simply two people who cared about each other, participating in community life, supporting local children, contributing to the fabric that made Sweetgum home for so many families.

"Mr. Khadir," Sarah Thompson tugged on his ghee sleeve. "Are we doing good?"

"You're doing perfectly," he said, returning his attention to his students. "Keep that posture, keep that spacing, keep that pride in what you've accomplished."

The parade route ended at the town square, where various organizations had set up informational booths and demonstrations. The dojo's booth featured photos from recent classes, information about their youth programs, and a small demonstration area where students could show basic techniques to interested families.

As the formal parade dissolved into the festival atmosphere, Khadir found himself genuinely enjoying the community celebration. Parents approached with questions about classes, kids demonstrated their newly learned skills for grandparents, and several teenagers who'd been considering martial arts training signed up for trial lessons.

"This was a good idea," Kiana said, watching Miguel patiently teach a break-fall to his younger sister. "Gets people thinking about us as community members instead of just that place where people learn to fight."

"That was always the goal."

Around noon, during a lull in the booth activity, Khadir spotted Naomi approaching with a cup of hot cider and a soft pretzel.

"Parade fuel," she said, offering to share. "You've been here all morning without a break."

"Thanks." He accepted half the pretzel gratefully. "How's the reading wagon going?"

"Twenty-seven new library card signups and counting. Plus I've had at least ten conversations about winter reading programs." She glanced around the festival, noting the easy way community members moved between booths, the relaxed atmosphere of neighbors catching up with neighbors. "This is nice. Normal in the best way."

"Normal is underrated."

"It really is." She paused, watching Omari demonstrate a technical stand-up for a couple of younger kids who were watching with obvious admiration. "He looks confident out there. Not just the physical techniques, but the way he carries himself."

"That's what good training does—builds confidence from the inside out."

A family approached the booth with questions about age requirements and class schedules, and Naomi stepped aside to let Khadir handle the business conversation. But she didn't go far, and he found himself aware of her presence throughout the interaction—the way she nodded encouragingly when he explained their approach to conflict resolution, the small smile when he talked about helping kids discover their own strength.

When the family left with a trial lesson scheduled for the following week, Naomi moved closer again.

"You're good at this," she observed. "The community outreach, the explaining without overselling."

"Years of practice. Though having community support makes it easier." He gestured toward the festival around them. "Six months ago, I wasn't sure how the dojo would be received. Whether people would see value in what we offer or just worry about teaching kids to fight."

"And now?"

"Now I think we've found our place. Part of the community fabric instead of separate from it."

As if to underscore his point, Mrs. Rodriguez approached with Miguel's little sister, who'd been pestering her parents about joining classes since watching Miguel's demonstration.

"Elena wants to know when she can start training," Mrs. Rodriguez said with an amused smile. "Apparently watching her brother isn't enough anymore."

"Age-appropriate classes start at six," Khadir said, crouching down to Elena's level. "But if you want to try some basics right now, I bet your brother would love to show you."

The impromptu lesson that followed—Miguel carefully teaching his sister a simple bow and basic stance—drew a small crowd of watching parents and children. The interaction was gentle, respectful, focused on building confidence rather than demonstrating dominance. Everything Khadir hoped his program would represent.

"That's exactly what people need to see," Naomi said quietly. "Kids teaching kids, families supporting each other, strength that looks like protection instead of aggression."

The afternoon continued in that vein—conversations with potential students, demonstrations of basic techniques, the kind of community building that happened naturally when people gathered to celebrate what they shared rather than focus on what divided them.

As the festival wound down, as booths were packed up and families headed home with balloons and memories, Khadir felt a deep sense of satisfaction settling in his chest. This was what he'd envisioned when he'd opened the dojo—not just a business, but a community resource. Not just instruction, but investment in the next generation's confidence and character.

"Good day?" Naomi asked as they helped students pack up the demonstration equipment.

"Very good day." He looked around the town square, noting the easy way his students interacted with other kids, the comfortable relationships they'd built with community families. "Feels like we've reached some kind of milestone."

"What kind of milestone?"

"The kind where we're not visitors anymore. We belong here."

As families began heading to their cars, as the festival atmosphere gave way to the quiet satisfaction of a community event well-executed, Khadir and Naomi found themselves walking together toward the parking area. Not hand-in-hand— they maintained appropriate public boundaries—but close enough for easy conversation, comfortable in each other's presence.

"Thank you," Naomi said as they reached the area where cars were parked.

"For what?"

"For being exactly who you are. For building something that makes this community better. For showing Omari and all these other kids what strength and leadership actually look like."

The gratitude in her voice made his chest tight with emotion. "Thank you for seeing it that way. For supporting it. For being part of it."

They stood together in the mild November afternoon, surrounded by the comfortable sounds of families loading up cars and making plans for the rest of their weekend. Normal sounds, ordinary moments, the kind of daily life that felt extraordinary when you were sharing it with the right person.

"See you Monday for class?" he asked.

"Wouldn't miss it."

As she drove away with Omari chattering in the backseat about the parade and the festival and his successful demonstrations, Khadir felt that familiar sense of rightness that had been growing stronger over the past months. This was what community looked like—not perfect, not without challenges, but real and supportive and worth the investment of time and care.

His phone buzzed with a text from Naomi:

Beautiful day. Proud to be part of what you're building. See you soon.

He typed back:

Proud to be building it with you.

Walking to his own car, Khadir looked back at the town square where families were finishing their cleanup, where kids were running around with the satisfied exhaustion that came from a day well-spent, where his students moved with the confident posture that spoke of lessons learned and community support.

Some days reminded you why the work mattered. This had been one of those days.

CHAPTER NINETEEN

Sunday morning arrived with the kind of domestic chaos that Naomi was learning to cherish. Omari had dumped half his bookshelf onto his bedroom floor while searching for a specific graphic novel, the coffee maker was making alarming gurgling sounds, and she couldn't find her reading glasses anywhere.

"Found them!" Omari called from the living room. "They're on top of the refrigerator!"

"Why would they be on top of the refrigerator?" she called back, abandoning the coffee maker to retrieve the glasses.

"Because you were putting away cereal and reading that book about teaching kids to be confident," he said matter-of-factly. "You always put things in weird places when you're multitasking."

The observation was uncomfortably accurate. She'd been reading everything she could find about child development and building resilience, partly for her work at the library and partly because watching Omari's transformation over the past months had made her curious about the science behind confidence-building.

Her phone buzzed with a text from Khadir:

> Good morning. Any interest in a domestic project today? I have a wobbly bookshelf that could use some expertise, and I bought too much tea for one person to drink.

She smiled, typing back:

> Omari's been complaining about his chapter books falling over. Maybe we could solve two problems at once?

> Perfect. Come over whenever you're ready. I'll provide the tools and the tea.

> Give us an hour to make ourselves presentable.

> You're always presentable.

An hour later, they stood in Khadir's living room examining the bookshelf in question—a tall, narrow unit that held his collection of martial arts texts, military history, and what appeared to be an impressive selection of mystery novels.

"It's not exactly wobbly," Omari observed, testing the stability with a gentle push. "It's more like... leaning."

"Definitely leaning," Naomi agreed. "Toward the window. Has it always done that?"

"It's gotten worse since I added the new books," Khadir said, pulling a small toolbox from the hall closet. "I think one of the wall anchors is coming loose."

What followed was the kind of pleasant domestic problem-solving that Naomi hadn't experienced since the early days of her marriage to Andre—back when they'd been partners in building a home instead of adversaries managing separate agendas.

Khadir was methodical and patient, explaining each step as he removed books and examined the mounting hardware. Omari proved surprisingly helpful, holding tools and asking thoughtful questions about why certain approaches worked better than others. And Naomi found herself genuinely enjoying the collaboration—three people working together toward a common goal without drama or competition.

"The anchor wasn't rated for this much weight," Khadir explained as he marked new drilling points. "I need to use something stronger and spread the load across more studs."

"Is that why my bookshelf keeps tipping over too?" Omari asked. "Because I keep adding more books?"

"Could be. We can check that next if you want."

The casual inclusion—*we can check that next*—made Naomi's chest warm. Not *your mom can figure it out* or *that's not my problem*, but the automatic assumption that helping was part of caring, that Omari's concerns were worth addressing.

While Khadir drilled new holes and installed heavy-duty anchors, Naomi organized his books into neat stacks, noting his reading preferences with interest.

"You have excellent taste in mysteries," she said, holding up a Louise Penny novel. "I keep recommending her to patrons who want smart, character-driven stories."

"She's brilliant at making you care about the whole community, not just the crime," he said, testing the stability of the newly secured shelf. "Plus Inspector Gamache reminds me of my favorite sergeant from the army—calm authority, patient with people's flaws, leads by example."

"Speaking of leading by example," Naomi said, watching Omari carefully hand tools back to Khadir without being asked, "you're teaching him more than just bookshelf repair."

"He's teaching me too. Kid notices details I miss and asks better questions than most adults."

They finished the project in companionable quiet, then

migrated to the kitchen where Khadir had indeed bought too much tea. The counter was lined with small tins bearing labels like "Evening Calm" and "Morning Focus" and "Rainy Day Comfort."

"I may have gotten carried away at the farmers market," he admitted. "The vendor was very persuasive about the benefits of having options."

"Options are good," Naomi said, examining the selection. "Especially when they come with excellent brewing instructions."

As she organized the tins in his cabinet—grouping them by type and time of day in a system that made intuitive sense—Omari wandered the kitchen, taking in details with his usual thoroughness.

"You have good snacks," he observed, noting the bowl of apples and the container of trail mix. "And your refrigerator is really organized."

"Military habits," Khadir said. "Once you learn to keep your gear squared away, everything else follows."

"Is that why the dojo is always so clean too?"

"Partly. But mostly because taking care of your training space is taking care of your training. Hard to focus on learning when you're surrounded by chaos."

Naomi listened to their easy conversation while she worked, noting the way Khadir answered Omari's questions with genuine attention, never talking down to him or dismissing his observations as unimportant. This was what she'd wanted for her son—adults who saw him as a complete person rather than just a small inconvenience or a project to be managed.

"There," she said, stepping back from the now-organized tea cabinet. "Everything labeled and arranged by caffeine content and time of day."

"That's incredibly helpful," Khadir said, studying her system with obvious appreciation. "And completely logical. Why didn't I think of that?"

"Because you're used to having one or two types of tea, not fifteen," she said pragmatically. "Once you have choices, you need systems."

They spent the rest of the morning in his backyard, where Omari helped Khadir rake leaves while Naomi sat on the back steps with a cup of "Autumn Comfort" tea and a book from his mystery collection. The domestic scene was so normal, so peacefully ordinary, that she found herself taking mental pictures—wanting to remember the way afternoon light slanted through the bare trees, the sound of Omari's laughter when he jumped in the leaf pile, the comfortable silence between conversation.

"This is nice," Omari said as they finally came inside, cheeks flushed from the cool air. "It feels like we're a family."

The comment hung in the air with the weight of hope and possibility. Naomi felt her heart skip, not with anxiety but with the recognition that yes, this did feel like family—the chosen kind, built on compatibility and affection rather than obligation.

"I like that feeling too," Khadir said quietly, meeting Naomi's eyes over Omari's head.

"Me too," she said. "Very much."

As they prepared to leave—gathering tools they'd borrowed, making sure they hadn't left anything behind—Naomi felt reluctant to break the spell of the afternoon. Not because going home was unpleasant, but because this easy togetherness felt so right, so sustainable, so much like the future she was beginning to let herself imagine.

"Next weekend," Khadir said as they stood by their cars, "there's a winter craft fair at the community center. Vendors, hot chocolate, probably some terrible folk music. Want to go together? All three of us?"

"That sounds perfect," Naomi said. "Omari loves craft fairs, and I love terrible folk music."

"It's a date then. A family date."

The phrase settled between them with quiet significance. They were past tentative courtship, past careful boundaries around Omari's involvement. They were building something intentional and inclusive, something that honored both the romantic connection between adults and the family unit they were creating together.

Driving home, Naomi found herself humming along to the radio while Omari chattered about bookshelf engineering and leaf pile physics and whether Mr. Khadir might want to help them organize his room too.

"He's good at fixing things," Omari observed. "And he doesn't get frustrated when stuff doesn't work the first time."

"Those are excellent qualities in a person."

"Are you going to marry him?"

The question was delivered with the same casual tone he'd used to discuss bookshelf stability, but Naomi felt her breath catch.

"We haven't talked about marriage yet," she said honestly. "But I love him, and I love the way we all are together."

"I love him too," Omari said matter-of-factly. "He listens to me like my ideas matter, and he makes you happy without making you worried all the time like Dad did."

The comparison was stark and accurate, and it reminded Naomi how much her son had absorbed during the difficult years of her marriage to Andre. But it also showed how clearly he could see the difference between relationships that diminished people and relationships that helped them grow.

"You're very wise for ten years old," she said.

"I pay attention," he said. "And I like what I see when I pay attention to you and Mr. Khadir together."

At home, they spent the evening organizing Omari's room

with the same systematic approach they'd used on Khadir's tea cabinet. Books arranged by reading level and series, art supplies sorted and accessible, everything in its proper place but not so rigid that creativity was stifled.

"There," Naomi said as they stepped back to admire their work. "Now your books won't fall over every time you pull one out."

"And I can find everything without dumping out all the drawers," Omari added with satisfaction. "Mr. Khadir was right about organization making everything easier."

As she tucked him into his newly organized room, Naomi felt a deep sense of contentment settling over her. This was what stability looked like—not the rigid control Andre had demanded, but the flexible structure that came from people caring about each other enough to build systems that worked for everyone.

"Sweet dreams," she said, kissing his forehead.

"Mom? Today was really good. Like, the best kind of regular day."

"I thought so too."

"Can we have more days like this?"

"I think we can," she said. "I think we're going to have a lot more days like this."

After he was asleep, she sat on her own bed and thought about the afternoon—the easy collaboration, the comfortable domestic rhythms, the way three separate people had functioned as a unit without anyone having to sacrifice their individual identity.

Her phone buzzed with a text from Khadir:

Thank you for today. For the bookshelf expertise, for the tea organization, for letting me be part of your Sunday.

She typed back:

Thank you for including us in your projects. For making ordinary tasks feel like adventures.

Every day with you feels like an adventure. The good kind.

The very best kind.

Sleep well. See you at class Tuesday.

Looking forward to it. Always.

Setting her phone aside, Naomi felt that familiar sense of rightness that had been growing stronger with each passing week. This was what love looked like when it was healthy—not desperate or possessive or conditional, but steady and supportive and expansive enough to include the people who mattered most.

Some days reminded you what you were building toward. Today had been one of those days.

CHAPTER TWENTY

Khadir was closing the dojo at 8:30 PM when he saw Andre Pierce standing across the street, partially hidden by the shadow of Justin Time's storefront. The man wasn't making any attempt at subtlety—just standing there, arms crossed, staring at the dojo with the kind of focused intensity that made every instinct Khadir had developed in the military go on high alert.

He finished his closing routine methodically—checking locks, setting the alarm, reviewing tomorrow's schedule with Kiana before she left through the back entrance. But his awareness stayed locked on the figure across the street, tracking movement and positioning the way he'd been trained to track potential threats.

When Khadir stepped outside and locked the front door, Andre began walking toward him.

"We need to talk," Andre said, his voice carrying across the quiet street.

"No, we don't." Khadir pocketed his keys and turned toward his car. "Any communication goes through Naomi, and any concerns about Omari go through proper channels."

"This is about my son's safety."

"Your son is perfectly safe. He's learning valuable skills from qualified instructors in a supervised environment."

Andre stepped closer, moving to block Khadir's path to his car. "He's learning violence from a man who's sleeping with his mother. You think that's appropriate?"

The words were designed to provoke, delivered with the kind of sneering confidence that suggested Andre had rehearsed this confrontation. Khadir felt his jaw tighten, but kept his voice level.

"I think Omari is learning confidence, respect, and practical life skills. I think his mother is an excellent judge of what's best for her son."

"His mother is thinking with her hormones instead of her brain." Andre moved closer still, close enough that Khadir could smell alcohol on his breath. "And you're taking advantage of a vulnerable woman and her child."

"Step back, please."

"Or what? You'll use your martial arts training on me? That would look great in a custody hearing—the violent instructor who attacked a concerned father."

The setup was transparent. Andre was trying to provoke a physical confrontation he could use as evidence of Khadir's unsuitability around children. But recognition of the trap didn't make it less dangerous—especially with alcohol lowering Andre's inhibitions and amplifying his aggression.

"I'm not going to fight you," Khadir said calmly. "I'm going to get in my car and leave. I suggest you do the same."

"You're going to stop seeing Naomi. You're going to stop teaching my son. You're going to get out of our lives before I make you get out."

The threats were escalating, the language becoming more explicitly menacing. Khadir pulled out his phone and started recording, holding it where Andre could see it.

"I'm documenting this conversation," he said clearly. "You're intoxicated, you're making threats, and you're blocking my access to my vehicle. I'm asking you once more to step back."

"Put that phone away." Andre's voice rose, and he moved closer instead of farther away. "You think you can record me? You think that scares me?"

"I think you should leave before you do something you'll regret."

"The only thing I regret is not handling this sooner."

Andre grabbed for the phone, and when Khadir pulled it back to protect it, Andre grabbed his wrist instead—the same wrist grab that Khadir taught students to escape from every week.

The irony wasn't lost on him.

"Let go," Khadir said, his voice carrying the kind of command authority he'd learned in the army.

"Make me."

It was exactly the wrong thing to say to someone with Khadir's training. But instead of escalating to strikes or throws, he used the same technique he taught in every beginners' class— a simple grip break that rotated toward Andre's thumb, the mechanically weakest part of his hold.

The grip popped open instantly, and Andre stumbled backward, off-balance and surprised.

"How did you—"

"Basic physics," Khadir said, stepping toward his car. "Same thing I teach ten-year-olds."

But Andre wasn't done. Whether from alcohol, wounded pride, or the realization that his intimidation tactics weren't working, he rushed forward and shoved Khadir hard in the chest.

Khadir had a split second to decide how to respond. He could have stepped aside and let Andre's momentum carry him past. He could have absorbed the push and simply walked away. Both options would have been tactically sound and legally defensible.

Instead, his protective instincts kicked in. Andre was drunk, aggressive, and clearly unstable. If he was willing to physically assault a trained martial artist in public, what might he do to Naomi in private? What had he already done during their marriage that she hadn't talked about?

When Andre shoved him, Khadir didn't step aside. He set his base, absorbed the impact, and when Andre tried to grab him again, he controlled the man's wrists and guided him firmly to the ground using a technique so basic it barely qualified as martial arts—just leverage and positioning and the kind of calm control that came from years of training.

Andre hit the pavement harder than Khadir had intended, the alcohol affecting his balance and ability to break his own fall. For a moment, he lay stunned, looking up at Khadir with surprise and something that might have been fear.

"Stay down," Khadir said quietly. "This is over."

But Andre wasn't staying down. He rolled to his feet, his face flushed with humiliation and rage, and reached into his jacket pocket.

"I'll show you what's over—"

"Hey!" The shout came from across the street, where Mrs. Patterson was walking her dog and had apparently been watching the entire confrontation. "Someone call 911!"

The presence of a witness changed everything. Andre's hand froze in his jacket, whatever he'd been reaching for forgotten in the face of potential legal consequences. Khadir stepped back, hands visible and non-threatening, still recording everything on his phone.

"Are you okay, Khadir?" Mrs. Patterson called, pulling out her own phone. "I saw the whole thing. That man attacked you."

"I'm fine, Mrs. Patterson. Thank you."

Sirens were audible in the distance—someone else had also called the police, or maybe Mrs. Patterson had already dialed. Andre looked around wildly, seeming to realize that his carefully planned confrontation had spiraled completely out of his control.

"This isn't over," he said, backing toward his car. "You have no idea what you've gotten yourself into."

"Yes, I do," Khadir said calmly. "I've gotten myself into a relationship with a wonderful woman and her son. Everything else is just noise."

The first police car arrived as Andre was getting into his vehicle. Officers separated them immediately—one taking Khadir's statement while another dealt with Andre, who was clearly intoxicated and increasingly belligerent as his adrenaline faded and the alcohol reasserted itself.

"You got it all on video?" Officer Martinez asked, reviewing the phone footage that clearly showed Andre as the aggressor.

"From the moment he made the first threat," Khadir confirmed. "He grabbed my wrist, shoved me, and was reaching for something in his jacket when Mrs. Patterson intervened."

"Good thinking on the recording. And good restraint—you could have hurt him badly if you'd wanted to."

"That was never the goal."

Mrs. Patterson gave her own statement, describing what she'd witnessed from across the street. Her account corroborated everything on Khadir's video—Andre as the aggressor, Khadir using minimal force in response, the escalating threats that had prompted her to call for help.

"We'll need you to come to the station tomorrow for a formal statement," Officer Martinez said as they wrapped up the scene. "And you should probably apply for a protective order. This guy's got warning signs written all over him."

As the police cars finally left—one with Andre in the back-seat, charged with assault and public intoxication—Khadir sat in his own car and tried to process what had happened. His hands were steady, his breathing controlled, but the adrenaline was starting to fade and leave him feeling hollow.

His phone buzzed with a text from Naomi:

> Just heard from Mrs. Patterson. Are you okay? Coming to the dojo now.

He typed back:

> Police just left. I'm fine. Meet you at my house instead?

> On my way.

Twenty minutes later, she was sitting on his couch while he made tea and told her everything that had happened. She listened without interrupting, her expression growing more tense as he described Andre's escalating threats and the physical confrontation that followed.

"I'm so sorry," she said when he finished. "This is my fault. I should have seen this coming, should have done more to protect you from his—"

"Naomi, stop." He set down his mug and moved to sit beside her. "This is not your fault. Andre made his own choices tonight. He chose to drink, chose to confront me, chose to make threats and get physical. Those are his decisions and his consequences."

"But if we weren't together, if I hadn't brought you into this mess—"

"If we weren't together, I wouldn't care as much about stopping him from hurting people. But we are together, and I do care, and I'm not sorry about that."

She leaned against him, and he could feel the tension in her shoulders, the way she was holding herself together through sheer will.

"What happens now?" she asked.

"Now Andre faces the consequences of assaulting someone in public while intoxicated. Now we file for protective orders. Now we document everything and let the legal system do its job."

"And us? Our relationship, Omari's training?"

"What about them?"

"Andre's going to use this. He'll say you're violent, that you attacked him, that you're dangerous around children." Her voice was tight with anxiety. "He'll twist everything to make himself the victim."

"Let him try. We have video evidence, witness statements, and a clear pattern of his escalating behavior." Khadir's voice was steady, certain. "Most importantly, we have the truth. And Omari knows the truth."

As if summoned by his name, her phone rang with a call from Mia's house, where Omari was spending the night.

"Hi, baby," she answered, putting it on speaker so Khadir could hear.

"Mom, Tyler's mom heard something happened with Dad and Mr. Khadir. Is everyone okay?"

The mature concern in his ten-year-old voice made Khadir's chest tight. This child had been forced to worry about adult problems for far too long.

"Everyone's okay," Naomi said. "Your father made some poor choices tonight, and there were consequences. Mr. Khadir is fine, I'm fine, and you don't need to worry about anything."

"Did Dad try to hurt Mr. Khadir?"

The directness of the question caught both adults off guard. But Omari had lived with Andre for years—he understood his father's capacity for intimidation and control better than anyone.

"Your father was angry about things that weren't his business," Khadir said gently. "He made some threats and got physical. But it's handled now, and everyone is safe."

"Are you going to keep teaching me? Even though Dad doesn't want you to?"

"As long as your mother wants me to teach you, and as long as you want to learn, yes. I'm not going anywhere."

"Good. Because I like learning from you, and I like how you make Mom happy."

After they hung up, Naomi was quiet for a long time, staring at her phone.

"He shouldn't have to worry about these things," she said finally. "He shouldn't have to manage his father's emotions or worry about whether the adults in his life are going to be there tomorrow."

"You're right. He shouldn't. But he does, and the best thing we can do is be consistent and honest with him. Show him what healthy relationships look like, teach him that love doesn't come with threats or conditions."

"Is that what we're doing? Showing him healthy love?"

"I think so. I hope so."

She curled up against his side, and they sat together in the quiet of his living room, processing the evening's events and what they meant for their future. Outside, Sweetgum settled into its nighttime rhythms—dogs barking, cars passing, the ordinary sounds of a community at rest.

"I love you," she said quietly.

"I love you too."

"Whatever comes next, we face it together?"

"Together," he confirmed. "Always together."

But even as he said the words, Khadir felt the weight of what Andre had set in motion tonight. The man had been looking for ammunition to use in a custody battle, and despite the video evidence and witness statements, he'd found it. A physical confrontation between his ex-wife's boyfriend and himself, regardless of who started it or how it ended, was exactly the kind of drama Andre could weaponize.

The fight was just beginning.

CHAPTER TWENTY-ONE

The custody modification paperwork arrived by certified mail on Tuesday morning, exactly forty-eight hours after Andre's arrest. Naomi signed for it with hands that only trembled slightly, then sat at her kitchen table and read through the legal language that was designed to sound reasonable and concerned while systematically attacking everything she'd built over the past year.

Petitioner requests modification of custody arrangement due to material changes in circumstances affecting the minor child's welfare and safety. Specifically: Mother's romantic involvement with martial arts instructor who has engaged in physical altercation with Petitioner; Mother's enrollment of minor child in potentially dangerous activities without Father's consent; Mother's demonstrated poor judgment regarding male influences in minor child's life.

The words blurred together as she read, each accusation a twisted version of reality designed to make her look unstable, reckless, unsafe. Andre was asking for primary custody, claiming that Omari was in danger from both the jiu-jitsu training and her relationship with Khadir.

Her phone rang before she could finish reading. Khadir's name on the screen.

"I got served too," he said without preamble. "At the dojo. He's named me as a co-respondent and is asking for a restraining order that would prevent me from having contact with Omari."

"Can he do that?"

"He can ask for it. Whether he'll get it depends on the judge and how well our lawyer can present the actual facts." His voice was steady, but she could hear the controlled anger underneath. "Naomi, I need to ask you something, and I need you to be completely honest."

Her stomach dropped. "What?"

"Are you having second thoughts about us? About whether fighting this battle is worth it?"

The question hit like cold water. "Why would you ask that?"

"Because I'm about to become a major liability in your custody case. Because Andre is going to paint me as a violent influence on your son, and some of that mud might stick despite the evidence. Because choosing to stay with me might cost you time with Omari."

She was quiet for a long moment, processing the weight of what he was saying. He was giving her an out, offering to step aside if she thought it would protect her relationship with her son.

"Khadir," she said finally, "do you remember what you told me that first night at the dojo? About learning to fall safely and get back up on purpose?"

"Yes."

"This feels like falling. Andre pushing us into this legal battle, making us defend our choices, threatening to take away what matters most." She looked around her kitchen—at Omari's artwork on the refrigerator, at the confidence cards they'd collected from the dojo, at the life they'd built together. "But I'm not afraid of falling anymore. I know how to get back up."

"What does that mean?"

"It means I love you. It means Omari loves you. It means what we have is worth fighting for, and I'm not going to let Andre's manipulation tactics destroy it." Her voice grew stronger with each word. "If he wants a custody battle, he can have one. But he's going to lose, because the truth is on our side."

The relief in Khadir's voice was audible. "I was hoping you'd say that."

"Were you really worried I'd choose differently?"

"I was worried you'd choose what felt safest instead of what felt right. There's a difference."

She understood exactly what he meant. Six months ago, she would have chosen safety—would have ended the relationship, pulled Omari from the dojo, tried to make herself small and invisible to avoid Andre's wrath.

But she wasn't that person anymore.

THAT EVENING, she sat Omari down for what she privately thought of as "the conversation"—the one where she had to explain that his father was trying to change their living arrangement, and why, and what it might mean for their family.

He listened with the serious expression he wore when processing difficult information, asking occasional questions but mostly just absorbing the reality of the situation.

"So Dad wants me to live with him instead of you?" he asked when she finished explaining.

"He's asking a judge to consider that, yes."

"Because he thinks Mr. Khadir is dangerous?"

"Because he's angry about choices I've made that he disagrees with."

Omari was quiet for a moment, swinging his legs from where he sat on the kitchen counter. "Can I tell the judge what I want?"

"Depending on how the case proceeds, you might have the opportunity to speak with a guardian ad litem—that's someone whose job is to represent what's best for you."

"And I can tell them I want to stay here? With you and Mr. Khadir?"

The casual way he included Khadir in their family unit made her throat tight. "You can tell them whatever you honestly feel."

"Good. Because I feel like Dad is being mean for no reason, and I don't want to live somewhere where people are mean for no reason."

The simple moral clarity of his ten-year-old perspective cut straight through all the legal complexity and emotional manipulation. Andre was being mean for no reason. Everything else was just noise.

"I'm scared about this, baby," she admitted. "I'm scared about what might happen, about having to fight for our family."

"Are you scared enough to give up?"

"No."

"Then I'm not scared either. Because you and Mr. Khadir are both really good at not giving up."

THE EMERGENCY HEARING was scheduled for the following Friday. Naomi spent the week in a strange state of suspended animation—going to work, teaching classes, maintaining normal routines while her lawyer prepared their defense and Andre's accusations hung over everything like storm clouds.

Khadir was dealing with his own legal challenges. Andre's

request for a restraining order meant he couldn't be alone with Omari until the hearing, couldn't teach him private lessons, couldn't even drive him home from group classes without another adult present. The restrictions felt arbitrary and punitive, designed more to disrupt their routine than to protect anyone.

"It's working," Naomi said Thursday night as they sat on her porch after Omari had gone to bed. "His strategy, I mean. Making everything feel complicated and fraught, making us question whether we're doing the right thing."

"Are you questioning it?"

"Every five minutes. But then I look at Omari—at how confident he's become, how happy he is, how much he's learned about standing up for himself—and I remember why we're fighting."

"What if we lose?" The question came out quietly, but it was the fear they'd both been carrying all week. "What if Andre convinces the judge that I'm a bad influence, that the jiu-jitsu training is inappropriate, that you're making poor choices?"

"Then we appeal. We keep fighting. We don't give up." She reached for his hand in the darkness. "But Khadir? I don't think we're going to lose. Because Andre's case is built on lies and manipulation, and ours is built on love and evidence."

"How can you be so certain?"

"Because I know what real harm looks like. I lived with it for years. And what we have—what we're building together—is the opposite of harm. It's healing."

Friday morning dawned clear and cold, the kind of November day that reminded you winter was coming whether you were ready or not. Naomi dressed carefully in her most professional outfit—the navy suit she wore to parent conferences and school board meetings, the one that made her look competent and responsible rather than dramatic or emotional.

At the courthouse, Andre was already waiting with his

lawyer, a sharp-faced woman who looked like she specialized in making reasonable requests sound urgent and necessary. Andre himself looked nothing like the angry, intoxicated man who'd confronted Khadir in the street. He was clean-shaven, conservatively dressed, every inch the concerned father who just wanted what was best for his son.

"He looks so... normal," Naomi whispered to her own attorney, a kind-faced woman named Susan Chen who specialized in family law.

"They always do," Susan replied. "That's why we stick to the facts and let the evidence speak for itself."

The hearing was mercifully brief. Andre's lawyer painted a picture of a mother making reckless choices, enrolling her son in dangerous activities, dating a violent man who had "physically assaulted" her client. She made it sound reasonable and protective, the natural concern of a father who'd witnessed alarming changes in his ex-wife's judgment.

Susan's response was methodical and devastating. She presented the video evidence from the night of the confrontation, showing clearly who had been the aggressor. She read from the police report, which documented Andre's intoxication and threatening behavior. She presented character witnesses who testified to both Naomi's and Khadir's positive influence on Omari's development.

Most importantly, she presented the documented pattern of Andre's escalating harassment—the anonymous social media posts (which had been traced back to his IP address), the inappropriate contact at Naomi's workplace, the threats and manipulation that had been carefully recorded and preserved.

"Your Honor," Susan concluded, "this is not a case about a mother making poor choices. This is a case about a father using the legal system to continue a pattern of control and intimidation that began during their marriage and has escalated since their divorce."

The judge—a stern-faced woman who looked like she'd seen every variation of family drama imaginable—reviewed the evidence with careful attention. When she finally spoke, her voice was measured but firm.

"Mr. Pierce, I find no evidence that your son is in any danger from his current living arrangement or activities. I do find evidence that you have been engaging in a pattern of harassment toward your ex-wife and her partner. The request for custody modification is denied. The request for a restraining order against Mr. Grant is denied."

Andre's face went tight with anger, but his lawyer placed a restraining hand on his arm before he could say anything that would make things worse.

"However," the judge continued, "I am issuing a protective order requiring Mr. Pierce to have no contact with Ms. Ellis outside of the court-approved co-parenting app, and no contact whatsoever with Mr. Grant. Any violation of this order will result in immediate legal consequences."

As they left the courthouse, Naomi felt lighter than she had in weeks. Not because the fight was over—Andre would undoubtedly appeal, would find new ways to cause trouble—but because the truth had been heard and acknowledged.

"How do you feel?" Susan asked as they stood on the courthouse steps.

"Like I can breathe again," Naomi said. "Like we chose the right thing, even when it was hard."

That afternoon, she and Omari went to the dojo for his regular class. For the first time in weeks, Khadir could work with him directly, could offer individual instruction, could be present as both teacher and caring adult without legal restrictions.

"I heard what happened in court," Omari said as he practiced his break-falls. "Mom told me we won."

"We did," Khadir confirmed. "The judge decided that you're exactly where you need to be."

"I'm glad. Because I like it here. I like learning from you and I like how happy Mom is and I like feeling like we're a family."

After class, the three of them went to Sweet and Spicy Chinese Palace for dinner—a small celebration of their legal victory and their continued ability to make choices about their own lives.

"To choosing what's right instead of what's easy," Naomi said, raising her glass of tea.

"To families that choose each other," Khadir added.

"To getting back up on purpose," Omari concluded, making both adults laugh.

Outside the restaurant, as they prepared to head to their separate cars, Khadir caught Naomi's hand.

"Thank you," he said quietly. "For fighting for us. For not giving up when it got difficult."

"Thank you for being worth fighting for."

As she drove home with Omari chattering in the backseat about his successful techniques and their celebratory dinner, Naomi felt a deep sense of peace settle over her. They had chosen love over fear, truth over manipulation, building something real over maintaining something broken.

Some battles were worth the cost of fighting them. This had been one of those battles.

CHAPTER TWENTY-TWO

The protective order hearing was scheduled for the following Tuesday, one week after the custody modification had been denied. Naomi sat on the courthouse steps at 8:30 AM, watching early morning traffic and trying to calm the nervous flutter in her stomach. Susan Chen had assured her this would be more straightforward than the custody hearing—they had clear evidence of Andre's harassment and the judge had already seen his pattern of behavior.

But court proceedings always felt unpredictable, and Andre had surprised them before.

"Ready for this?" Khadir asked, settling beside her on the cold stone steps.

"As ready as anyone can be for legally documenting that their ex-husband is a stalker," she said, then immediately felt bad for the sarcasm. "Sorry. I'm nervous."

"You're allowed to be nervous. This is a big step."

She looked at him—solid, steady, dressed in the same navy suit he'd worn to the custody hearing. Over the past week, as they'd prepared for this moment, she'd watched him handle the stress and uncertainty with remarkable grace. Never pressuring her to make decisions faster than she was ready for, never making her feel guilty for the complications her past had brought into his life.

"I keep thinking about what would have happened if I'd recognized your love back then," she said. "Instead of being swept away by Andre."

"You wouldn't have been you. You'd have been someone else—someone who hadn't learned to recognize manipulation, hadn't developed the strength to set boundaries, hadn't figured out what she actually wanted from life."

The observation was characteristically thoughtful. "You think all of this made me better?"

"I think all of this made you stronger. There's a difference."

Susan Chen appeared at the courthouse entrance, looking professional and confident in a way that made Naomi feel more optimistic about their chances.

"Good morning," she said, joining them on the steps. "How are we feeling?"

"Nervous but determined," Naomi said.

"Perfect attitude. I've reviewed the evidence again this morning, and we have a strong case. Andre's behavior meets the legal definition of harassment, and the documentation you've kept has been thorough and consistent."

They walked into the courthouse together, through security and up to the family court floor. The familiar institutional smell—cleaning products and nervous sweat and old coffee—made Naomi's stomach clench with remembered anxiety from her divorce proceedings two years earlier.

But this time felt different. This time, she wasn't asking for permission to leave an abusive situation—she was asking for legal protection to maintain the healthy life she'd built.

Andre was already there with his lawyer, the same sharp-faced woman from the custody hearing. He looked smaller somehow in the courthouse's fluorescent lighting, less intimidating than he'd seemed in the past. Just a man in an ill-fitting suit, trying to control something that was no longer his to control.

The hearing began with Susan presenting their evidence methodically. Screenshots of Andre's harassing text messages. Documentation of his appearance at Naomi's workplace after hours. The police report from his confrontation with Khadir. The IP address evidence linking him to the anonymous social media posts.

"Your Honor," Susan concluded, "Ms. Ellis has provided clear and convincing evidence that Mr. Pierce has engaged in a pattern of harassment that has escalated over time. She is requesting a protective order not out of vindictiveness, but out of genuine concern for her safety and the safety of her son."

Andre's lawyer tried to reframe the evidence as "concerned co-parenting" and "miscommunications between divorced parents." She painted Andre as a devoted father who was simply worried about his son's welfare and frustrated by his ex-wife's refusal to communicate effectively.

"Mr. Pierce has never physically harmed Ms. Ellis," she argued. "His attempts to discuss their son's welfare have been mischaracterized as harassment. A protective order is unnecessary and would interfere with his parental rights."

The judge—the same stern woman who'd handled their custody hearing—listened to both sides with the same careful attention she'd shown before. When Andre's lawyer finished, she reviewed the evidence file in silence for what felt like an eternity.

"Mr. Pierce," she said finally, "approach the bench."

Andre stood and walked forward, his lawyer beside him. Naomi couldn't hear what the judge said, but she could see Andre's face tightening as he listened. When they returned to the defendant's table, he looked angry but subdued.

"Based on the evidence presented," the judge announced, "I

find that Mr. Pierce has engaged in a pattern of harassment that meets the legal standard for a protective order. Specifically, his after-hours appearance at Ms. Ellis's workplace, his excessive and threatening communications, and his physical confrontation with her romantic partner demonstrate an escalating pattern of behavior that poses a credible threat."

Naomi felt her shoulders relax for the first time all morning.

"Therefore, I am granting a two-year protective order with the following terms: Mr. Pierce is prohibited from any direct contact with Ms. Ellis outside of the court-approved co-parenting application. He is prohibited from appearing at her workplace, her residence, or any location where she is present outside of scheduled custody exchanges. He is prohibited from any contact whatsoever with Mr. Grant."

The judge's voice carried the authority of someone who'd seen too many cases where harassment escalated to violence, who understood the importance of clear legal boundaries.

"Violation of this order will result in immediate arrest and criminal charges. Do you understand these terms, Mr. Pierce?"

"Yes, Your Honor," Andre said, his voice tight with barely controlled anger.

"Good. Court is adjourned."

As they gathered their papers and prepared to leave, Naomi felt a surge of relief so strong it made her dizzy. Two years. Two years of legal protection, of clear boundaries, of consequences if Andre chose to continue his harassment.

On the courthouse steps, Susan shook both their hands with genuine satisfaction.

"That went exactly as well as we could have hoped," she said. "The judge clearly understood the seriousness of the situation and the need for protection."

"What happens now?" Khadir asked.

"Now you live your lives," Susan said simply. "Andre has been put on legal notice that his behavior is unacceptable and will have consequences. If he violates the order, call the police immediately—don't try to handle it yourselves."

As Susan walked away to her next appointment, Naomi and Khadir stood together on the courthouse steps, looking out at the ordinary Tuesday morning activity of downtown Sweetgum. Cars passing, people heading to work, the normal rhythm of a community going about its business.

"How do you feel?" Khadir asked.

"Free," she said, and was surprised by how true it felt. "For the first time in years, I feel completely free to make my own choices without worrying about Andre's reaction."

"What do you want to do with that freedom?"

She thought about the question as they walked toward their cars. What did she want to do with a life that was finally, fully her own to direct?

"I want to keep building what we're building," she said. "I want to watch Omari continue growing into the confident, kind person he's becoming. I want to expand the reading programs at the library. I want to wake up every morning knowing that the people in my life are there because they choose to be, not because they're trying to control or manage me."

"Those sound like excellent goals."

"What about you? How do you feel?"

"Relieved," he said immediately. "But also... hopeful. Like we can finally stop reacting to Andre's drama and start focusing on our own future."

They'd reached their cars, parked side by side in the courthouse lot. In a few hours, they'd both be back to their regular routines—him at the dojo, her at the library, Omari at school. Normal life, protected now by legal boundaries and official recognition that what they'd built together was worth protecting.

"Khadir," she said as they stood between their cars.

"Yes?" he asked, looking at her gently.

"Thank you for staying. For fighting for us when it would have been easier to walk away," she said earnestly.

"I'll always fight for you."

He leaned down and kissed her—nothing dramatic or passionate, just the soft, familiar affection of two people who'd weathered a storm together and come out stronger. When they broke apart, they were both smiling.

"See you tonight for class?" he asked.

"Wouldn't miss it."

As she drove back to Sweetgum Elementary for her regular workday, Naomi felt a lightness she looked forward to getting used to. The protective order was more than just a legal document—it was official recognition that she had the right to live her life without harassment, that her choices were valid, that the family she was building with Khadir and Omari was legitimate and worth protecting.

Her phone buzzed with a text from Omari, sent from school:

> Tyler's mom heard about court. Did we win again?

She typed back:

> Yes, baby. We won again.

> Good. Can we have Chinese food tonight to celebrate?

> Absolutely.

> I love you, Mom.

> I love you too.

At the next red light, she took a moment to really look around at the town she'd chosen to call home. The familiar storefronts, the community members she'd come to know, the place where she'd learned to be strong and where her son was learning the same lesson.

This was what victory looked like—not dramatic or cinematic, but quiet and solid and sustainable. Legal protection for the life she'd built, community support for the choices she'd made, and the knowledge that she'd chosen love and truth over fear and manipulation.

Some battles ended not with grand gestures, but with the simple right to wake up each morning and choose your own life. Today, she'd won that right for herself and her family.

It felt like everything.

The next Confidence & Kindness Night fell on the first Saturday in December, exactly six weeks after the original event that had brought so many families into the dojo for the first time. The intervening weeks—filled with custody hearings, protective orders, and legal drama—felt like ancient history now that they were setting up folding chairs and arranging book displays again.

"Feels different this time," Kiana observed as she tested the microphone they'd borrowed from the community center. "More settled. Like we belong here instead of trying to prove ourselves."

"That's exactly how it feels," Naomi agreed, arranging the reading corner with the same care she'd taken the first time, but without the nervous energy that had accompanied her initial efforts. Tonight, she knew these families, knew which children would gravitate toward which books, knew that her presence here was welcomed rather than tolerated.

Khadir was setting up demonstration mats with help from several of his regular students, including Omari, who'd been promoted to orange belt the week before and wore his new rank with obvious pride.

"Mr. Khadir," Sarah Thompson called from where she was practicing her break-falls, "are we going to do the same techniques as last time?"

"Some of the same, some new ones," he replied. "Tonight we're going to focus on 'standing up on purpose'—getting to your feet with intention instead of just scrambling up however you can."

"Like the technical stand-up?" Miguel Rodriguez asked, demonstrating the movement they'd been practicing in class.

"Exactly like that. But tonight, we're going to talk about what it means beyond just the physical technique."

By 6 PM, the dojo was filled with familiar faces and several new ones. Families who'd attended the original event had brought friends and neighbors. Parents who'd been considering martial arts for their children had finally decided to give it a try. The atmosphere was warm and welcoming, filled with the kind of community energy that made events like this feel more like family gatherings than formal demonstrations.

"Welcome back, everyone," Khadir said once the crowd had settled. "And welcome to those of you joining us for the first time. Six weeks ago, we talked about confidence and kindness, and how they work together to help us move through the world with strength and compassion."

He paused, looking around at the assembled faces—parents and children, teenagers and grandparents, the diverse mix of community members who'd chosen to spend their Saturday evening learning something new together.

"Tonight, we want to add another concept: standing up on purpose. What does it mean to get back on your feet with intention? How do we turn falling down from something that happens to us into something we can manage and recover from?"

Naomi watched from the reading corner as he began the demonstration, noting the way the crowd leaned forward with interest, the way children automatically moved closer to get a better view. This was Khadir at his best—teaching not just physical techniques but life lessons, helping people understand that strength came from how you responded to challenges rather than from avoiding them altogether.

"First, let's talk about falling safely," he said, settling onto the mat. "Anyone remember the key principles from last time?"

Hands shot up throughout the audience. Mrs. Rodriguez called out, "Protect your head!" while one of the teenagers added, "Spread out the impact so it doesn't all hit one spot!"

"Perfect. Now watch what happens when I combine a safe fall with an intentional recovery."

He demonstrated the sequence they'd been practicing in class—the break-fall followed immediately by the technical stand-up, one fluid movement that took him from falling backward to standing ready in less than three seconds.

"That looked easy," someone called from the back.

"It is easy once you practice it enough," Khadir replied. "But more importantly, it's powerful. When you know you can fall safely and get back up quickly, you stop being afraid of taking risks. You stop being afraid of trying new things."

As the demonstration continued, Naomi found herself thinking about her own journey over the past six months. The first tentative steps into the dojo, the gradual building of physical confidence, the way learning to fall safely had translated into learning to take emotional risks. Standing up on purpose— it was a perfect metaphor for everything she'd learned about rebuilding her life after divorce.

"Ms. Naomi," a small voice said beside her. "Can you read us the book about being brave?"

She looked down to find Elena Rodriguez, Miguel's little

sister, holding a picture book about a mouse who learned to speak up for herself.

"Of course," Naomi said, settling into the reading chair. "Who else wants to hear about Mimi the Brave Mouse?"

Half a dozen children gathered on the floor cushions, ranging in age from five to ten. As she read, Naomi was aware of the parallel lessons happening throughout the dojo—physical techniques being taught on the mats, stories about courage and kindness being shared in the reading corner, families learning together that strength came in many different forms.

When she finished the story, Elena raised her hand. "Ms. Naomi, are you brave like Mimi?"

The question caught her off guard, not because she didn't know how to answer it, but because she realized she did know— with a certainty that would have been impossible six months ago.

"I'm learning to be brave," she said. "Just like Mimi had to practice speaking up, I've had to practice standing up for myself and making choices that feel right, even when they're scary."

"Like dating Mr. Khadir even though some people said mean things about it?"

Out of the mouths of babes. "Yes, like that. Sometimes being brave means continuing to do what you know is right even when other people disagree."

"And like my mom coming to live here even though she was scared about starting over?"

That came from Tyler, Mia's nephew, whose mother had recently moved to Sweetgum after her own difficult divorce.

"Exactly like that. Being brave doesn't mean you're not scared—it means you do important things even when you are scared."

As the reading corner discussion continued, the main demonstration was wrapping up with families trying the basic techniques themselves. Naomi watched Omari help younger children with their break-falls, noting the patient way he explained the positioning, the encouragement he offered when someone struggled with the movement.

"He's good at that," Khadir said, appearing beside her as the evening wound down. "Teaching, I mean. He has the right instincts for it."

"He's learned from watching you. The patience, the way you break things down into manageable steps, the encouragement without false praise."

"He's learned from watching you too. The way you match people with exactly what they need, the way you see potential in everyone."

As families began packing up and saying their goodbyes, several parents approached Naomi with questions about book recommendations, reading programs, and resources for children who learned differently. The conversations felt natural and easy, part of her established role in the community rather than something she had to prove herself worthy of.

"Same time next month?" Mrs. Thompson asked as she helped Sarah gather her things.

"Absolutely," Khadir confirmed. "We're thinking about adding a potluck element—make it even more of a community gathering."

"That sounds wonderful. Sarah's been asking about it every day since we got home from the last one."

After the last family left, Naomi, Khadir, Kiana, and Omari worked together to clean up the space. The routine was comfortable now, each person knowing their role, the work getting done efficiently through practiced teamwork.

"This was even better than the first one," Kiana said as she stacked the borrowed chairs. "More relaxed, more connected. Like we've all grown into ourselves a bit more."

"I felt that too," Naomi said. "Less nervous energy, more genuine connection."

As they finished the cleanup, Omari approached the front of the room where a small podium stood—left over from the microphone setup.

"Can I say something?" he asked, looking between the adults. "Like a speech?"

"Of course," Khadir said. "What's on your mind?"

Omari climbed onto the small platform and looked out at his audience of three, suddenly serious in the way children became when they had something important to communicate.

"Six months ago, I was scared of a lot of things," he began, his voice clear in the quiet dojo. "I was scared of kids at school, scared of trying new things, scared of standing up for myself. I felt small and invisible and like I didn't matter very much."

Naomi felt her throat tighten with emotion, but she stayed quiet, letting him find his words.

"Then Mom brought me here, and Mr. Khadir taught me how to fall down safely and get back up on purpose. He taught me that being strong doesn't mean being mean, and that confidence comes from knowing you can handle whatever happens."

He paused, looking directly at his mother with the kind of intense sincerity that only children could manage.

"But the most important thing I learned wasn't from the jiu-jitsu. It was from watching Mom get braver and happier. She stopped being scared of Dad's angry messages. She stopped apologizing for making good choices. She stopped making herself small so other people would feel comfortable."

Tears were flowing freely down Naomi's cheeks now, but she made no move to wipe them away.

"So I wanted to say thank you," Omari continued, "for showing me what it looks like to stand up on purpose. Not just with your body, but with your whole life. For choosing to be happy even when it was hard. For teaching me that families can be people who choose each other and make each other better."

He climbed down from the platform and walked directly to

Naomi, wrapping his arms around her waist in the kind of fierce hug that said everything words couldn't capture.

"I'm proud of you, Mom. And I'm proud of us."

"I'm proud of you too, baby," she managed through her tears. "So proud I can barely stand it."

Khadir and Kiana were both crying now too, moved by the simple eloquence of a ten-year-old's perspective on courage and family and the power of choosing to stand up on purpose.

"That," Kiana said, wiping her eyes, "is exactly why we do this work."

"That," Khadir added, "is what confidence and kindness look like when they grow up together."

As they finally locked up the dojo and prepared to head home, Naomi felt a deep sense of completion settling over her. Not the completion that came from ending something, but the kind that came from fully inhabiting your life, from becoming the person you were meant to be.

"Hungry?" Khadir asked as they reached their cars. "Mrs. Zhang left a message saying she has extra lo mein if we want to pick it up."

"Always hungry for Mrs. Zhang's lo mein," Omari said immediately.

"Sweet and Spicy Chinese Palace it is," Naomi said. "But first —" She turned to face both of them in the parking lot. "I want to say something too."

They waited, patient and attentive.

"Six months ago, I thought I was just looking for a way to help my son feel more confident. I had no idea I was actually looking for a way to feel more confident myself. I had no idea I was looking for family, for community, for the kind of love that makes you bigger instead of smaller."

She reached for Khadir's hand, then for Omari's, linking the three of them together in the quiet parking lot.

"Thank you for seeing who I could become before I knew it

myself. Thank you for teaching me that standing up on purpose isn't just about physical technique—it's about choosing courage over comfort, growth over safety, love over fear."

"Thank you for choosing us," Khadir said quietly. "For fighting for us when it would have been easier to give up."

"Thank you for being the best family ever," Omari added with the straightforward honesty that made adults wish they could see the world through ten-year-old eyes.

As they drove through downtown Sweetgum toward Sweet and Spicy Chinese Palace, Naomi looked around at the familiar storefronts, the community she'd claimed as home, the life she'd built through a series of small, brave choices. This was what standing up on purpose looked like in real life—not dramatic gestures or grand declarations, but the daily decision to choose growth, to choose love, to choose the people and activities and values that made you proud of who you were becoming.

Some stories ended with the characters getting exactly what they'd always wanted. But the best stories, Naomi reflected, ended with the characters becoming people who were worthy of what they'd received—people who could appreciate love because they'd learned to love themselves, who could build healthy relationships because they'd learned to set boundaries, who could teach courage because they'd learned to practice it themselves.

Tonight felt like the end of one story and the beginning of another. Both felt exactly right.

CHAPTER TWENTY-FOUR

Spring came early to Sweetgum that year, arriving in mid-March with warm breezes and the kind of golden afternoon light that made everyone want to spend time outdoors. Khadir had been thinking about timing for weeks— not the grand gesture kind of timing that involved flash mobs or skywriting, but the ordinary, meaningful kind that happened when life created perfect, quiet moments.

Omari was at chess club with Tyler and Mia's family, a Thursday evening tradition that had developed over the winter months. Naomi was meeting with parents about the library's summer reading program, which meant she'd be finished around seven and would likely want to decompress with a walk before heading home.

He'd suggested they meet at Roasted Beans after her meeting, then walk the route that had become familiar over the past months—past Justin Time's watch repair, past Sweet and Spicy Chinese Palace, past the community garden where Mrs. Williams was already planning her spring planting.

What he hadn't mentioned was the small velvet box in his jacket pocket, or the conversation he'd had with Omari two weeks earlier about what it meant to ask someone to marry you, and whether a ten-year-old thought his mother might be ready for that particular question.

"She talks about future stuff a lot now," Omari had said with his characteristic directness. "Like where we might go for vacation this summer, or whether we should plant a garden in the backyard, or how she wants to expand the reading programs next year. She didn't used to do that."

"What do you think that means?"

"I think it means she's not scared about what might happen anymore. She's excited about it."

Out of the mouths of babes.

Now, walking slowly down Pine Street with Naomi's hand warm in his, Khadir felt the weight of the ring and the lightness of absolute certainty. Nine months of getting to know each other again, nine months of building something real and sustainable, nine months of proving to themselves and their community that love could be steady and supportive instead of dramatic and exhausting.

"How was the meeting?" he asked as they paused to let Mrs. Patterson's dog complete his elaborate investigation of a particularly interesting fire hydrant.

"Better than expected. Fifteen families signed up for the summer program, and three parents volunteered to help with special events." She smiled up at him. "Mrs. Rodriguez wants to organize a bilingual story time, and the Thompsons offered to help with the outdoor reading sessions in the park."

"That sounds wonderful. Like the community is really embracing the expanded programs."

"It feels that way. Like we've moved past just providing basic services to actually creating something special." She paused. "Kind of like everything else this year—building something that's better than what came before."

They continued walking, past the shops that had become

familiar landmarks in their shared geography. The spring evening was perfect—warm but not humid, busy but not crowded, filled with the comfortable sounds of a small town settling into its evening rhythms.

"Naomi," Khadir said as they reached the town square, where the gazebo stood surrounded by early daffodils and the promise of more flowers to come.

"Yes?"

"Can we sit for a minute? There's something I want to ask you."

She looked at him with mild curiosity, probably expecting a question about weekend plans or summer schedules or some other practical aspect of their shared life. When he guided her to the same bench where they'd shared their first kiss all those months ago, her expression shifted to something more attentive.

"This feels significant," she said, settling beside him.

"It is significant." He turned to face her fully, noting the way the evening light caught the natural curl of her hair, the warmth in her dark eyes, the patient expression of someone who'd learned to trust that whatever came next would be handled with care and consideration.

"Nine months ago," he began, "you walked into my dojo looking for a way to help your son feel more confident. I don't think either of us expected to find what we found."

"Which was?"

"Partnership. The real kind—where both people become better versions of themselves instead of smaller ones. Where love feels like expansion instead of contraction. Where family means people who choose each other and work to deserve that choice every day."

Her breath caught slightly, and he could see understanding dawning in her expression.

"Naomi Ellis," he said, pulling the ring box from his pocket and opening it to reveal the simple solitaire he'd chosen—elegant but not ostentatious, classic but not old-fashioned, exactly right for a woman who valued substance over spectacle. "Will you marry me?"

The question hung in the evening air between them, surrounded by the ordinary sounds of their chosen community. Somewhere nearby, children were playing in the park. A dog barked once and then quieted. Cars passed with the unhurried pace of people heading home from work or errands or the small activities that made up a life.

"Yes," she said, and the word came out soft and sure and filled with the kind of joy that made her whole face light up. "Yes, absolutely yes."

He slipped the ring onto her finger—a perfect fit, thanks to Omari's covert intelligence gathering about his mother's jewelry size—and then he was kissing her, right there on the bench where they'd first admitted their feelings for each other.

When they broke apart, they were both crying and laughing, overwhelmed by the simple perfection of the moment and what they were promising each other.

"I love you," she said through her tears. "I love you so much, and I love the life we're building, and I love that you asked me here, in this place that's become ours."

"I love you too. I love your strength and your kindness and the way you see potential in everyone. I love being part of your team with Omari, and I love the family we're creating together."

They sat together as the sun set over Sweetgum, talking quietly about timing and ceremonies and all the practical details that came with deciding to officially commit your lives to each other. But mostly, they just sat close together, absorbing the reality of this new chapter, this new level of certainty and commitment.

"How long have you been planning this?" Naomi asked, admiring the ring on her finger.

"The proposal? About a month. The wanting to propose? Probably since our second date."

"What made you choose tonight?"

"Omari said something about how you talk about future plans now instead of just getting through each day. It made me realize that we'd moved from surviving to thriving, from hoping things would work out to knowing they would."

"He's very wise for ten years old."

"He gets that from his mother."

As they finally stood to head home—to collect Omari from chess club, to share their news, to begin the process of planning a wedding that would celebrate not just their love but the family they'd built together—Naomi felt a deep sense of rightness settling over her.

This was what happily ever after actually looked like—not a fairy tale ending, but a beginning. Not perfection, but the promise to keep choosing each other through whatever came next. Not the absence of challenges, but the confidence that they could handle those challenges together.

"One more thing," Khadir said as they reached their cars. "Omari already knows. I asked his permission before I bought the ring."

"You asked his permission?"

"I asked if he thought you might be ready, and if he'd be okay with me officially joining the family. He said yes to both questions, then gave me a very serious lecture about the importance of treating you like the treasure you are."

"That sounds like him."

"He also said he's been waiting for you to have a ring so he could tell people at school that his stepdad teaches martial arts."

The casual way he said "stepdad" made her heart skip with pure joy. Not "mom's boyfriend" or "mom's friend" but the word that acknowledged what Khadir had already become in Omari's life—a father figure, a mentor, a permanent part of their family structure.

"I think," she said, rising on her toes to kiss him one more time, "this is going to be the best adventure yet."

"I think so too."

As they drove through downtown Sweetgum toward the community center where Omari was undoubtedly winning at chess and probably organizing everyone else's pieces too, Khadir looked at the ring on Naomi's finger and felt the truth of what they'd committed to settling into his chest.

EPILOGUE

Six months later, Naomi stood at the back of the dojo watching Omari tie his new green belt around his waist with the careful precision he brought to everything that mattered to him. Stripe day had evolved into something of a community celebration over the past year, with families gathering to witness promotions and share in the quiet pride that came from watching children achieve goals they'd worked toward with patience and dedication.

"That's a good look on him," Mia said, appearing beside her with two cups of Mrs. Zhang's hot chocolate. "The belt, but also the confidence. Kid stands completely different than he did a year ago."

"He is completely different," Naomi agreed, accepting the warm cup gratefully. "Still thoughtful and careful, but not worried all the time. Not braced for the next crisis."

They watched as Omari demonstrated his newly learned technique—a smooth combination of movements that flowed from defensive positioning to safe distance creation to ready stance. The same progression Naomi had learned in her own first months of training, but executed now with the fluid competence that came from regular practice and genuine understanding.

"Beautifully done," Khadir said, and Naomi heard the pride in his voice that had nothing to do with martial arts technique and everything to do with watching a child he'd come to love reach a milestone through his own hard work.

The small reading corner that had been part of the dojo's community events was now a permanent fixture, marked by a hand-painted sign that read "Ellis Family Picks." Families regularly browsed the carefully curated selection of books about courage, friendship, and overcoming challenges—titles that Naomi refreshed seasonally and restocked based on what children actually checked out and talked about.

"The reading corner was inspired," Kiana said, joining their small group of observers. "Half these kids discovered they actually like reading because you found exactly the right books for their interests."

"And the other half discovered that their parents like reading to them more when the books are actually engaging," Naomi added, watching Mrs. Rodriguez settle into the reading chair with her youngest daughter and a picture book about a girl who learned to speak up for herself.

The ceremony continued with other promotions—Sarah Thompson earning her yellow belt, Miguel Rodriguez advancing to orange, several new students receiving their first stripes. Each advancement was celebrated with the same genuine enthusiasm, each child's progress acknowledged as worthy of community attention and pride.

"And finally," Khadir announced as the formal promotions concluded, "we have some news to share that probably isn't news to anyone who lives in Sweetgum."

Naomi felt her stomach flutter with pleasant nervousness, though she had to smile at his acknowledgment of small-town reality.

"Naomi and I were married two weeks ago," Khadir said, his arm sliding around her waist in the gesture that had become as natural as breathing. "Right here in the town square, with what felt like half the community in attendance. But for those who couldn't make it, we wanted you to know how much your support has meant to us."

The applause was immediate and genuine, accompanied by cheers from the kids and knowing smiles from the parents who'd been speculating about wedding plans since the engagement announcement.

"Speech!" Miguel called out, and the cry was taken up by several other students.

"Oh no," Naomi said, laughing. "I don't do speeches."

"Sure you do," Omari said, appearing at her elbow with the confidence of someone who'd recently been promoted and felt capable of managing all social situations. "You give book talks all the time. This is just a different kind of book talk."

"About what?"

"About the story you and Khadir are writing together."

The simplicity of his framing made something click into place for her. This was a story—not the dramatic kind with villains and rescues and grand gestures, but the quiet kind about people who choose each other and do the daily work of building something lasting.

"Eleven months ago," she began, speaking to the assembled families who'd become part of their extended community, "I brought Omari here because I needed help—help giving him confidence, help teaching him to stand up for himself, help figuring out how to be the parent he deserved."

She paused, looking around at the faces that had become familiar over months of shared classes and community events.

"What I found was more help than I'd asked for. I found a place where both of us could learn to be stronger without having to be harder. Where we could practice falling safely and getting back up with purpose. Where we discovered that family isn't just something you're born into—it's something you choose and nurture and earn through consistency and care."

Omari was beaming at her with the kind of uncomplicated pride that made her chest tight with emotion.

"So thank you," she continued, "for being part of our story. For showing up, for celebrating our victories, for teaching us that community support isn't just about the big moments—it's about the ordinary Tuesday evenings when you choose to spend time helping each other get a little bit stronger."

The applause was warm and sustained, but what meant more to Naomi was the way people came up afterward—not to offer congratulations exactly, but to share their own stories about what the dojo community had meant to their families. Parents talking about children who'd found confidence, kids describing how they'd handled challenging situations using skills learned on these mats, families who'd built friendships through shared commitment to growth and mutual support.

As the evening wound down and families began heading home with the satisfied tiredness that came from meaningful time spent together, Naomi found herself in the reading corner, straightening books and updating the recommendation cards that helped parents choose appropriate titles for their children's interests and reading levels.

"Leave it," Khadir said, settling beside her on the floor cushions. "It'll still be here tomorrow."

"I know. I just like making sure everything's organized for next time." She looked around the space that had become so central to her sense of purpose and belonging. "Hard to believe it's only been eleven months since I first walked through those doors."

"Eleven months since you walked through those doors terrified and desperate and trying to solve everyone's problems but your own," he corrected gently.

"And now?"

"Now you walk through those doors like you own the place. Because in all the ways that matter, you do."

Omari appeared from the equipment room where he'd been helping Kiana organize training gear, still wearing his new green belt and the satisfied expression of someone who'd accomplished something worth working toward.

"Ready to go home?" he asked.

"Ready," Naomi confirmed, gathering her things and turning off the lights in the reading corner.

As they locked up the dojo and walked to their cars—Omari chattering about his promotion requirements for the next level, making plans for weekend training sessions, discussing which of his school friends might be interested in trying a beginner class—Naomi felt the deep contentment that came from living a life that aligned with your values.

This was what happily ever after looked like in real life. Not perfect, not dramatic, not free from challenges or uncertainty. But grounded in mutual respect, sustained by community support, strengthened by the daily choice to keep showing up for each other.

"Ice cream?" Khadir suggested as they reached the parking area. "To celebrate the new belt?"

"Always ice cream for new belts," Omari said immediately. "It's tradition."

"Scoop! There It Is! it is," Naomi said, climbing into her car.

As they drove through downtown Sweetgum toward their celebratory ice cream, Naomi caught sight of her reflection in the rearview mirror and was struck by how different she looked from the anxious, uncertain woman who'd first sought help for her son's confidence issues. Not physically different—though she did stand straighter, move with more assurance—but fundamentally different in the way she inhabited her own life.

She looked like someone who knew her own worth.

Someone who'd learned to ask for what she needed and accept what she deserved. Someone who'd discovered that love didn't have to be complicated or conditional, that strength didn't require hardness, that family was built through choices made consistently over time.

Her phone buzzed with a text from Mia:

> Proud of you both tonight. See you for coffee tomorrow?

She typed back:

> Wouldn't miss it. Thank you for being part of our story.

> Thank you for letting me be part of it.

At Scoop! There It Is!, they ordered their usual celebration treats and found their familiar table by the window. As Omari described his promotion test in detail and Khadir offered gentle corrections to his technique descriptions, Naomi allowed herself a moment of quiet gratitude for the series of small, brave choices that had led to this ordinary, perfect evening.

Some stories ended with weddings or victories or dramatic resolutions. But the best stories, she'd learned, were the ones that ended with the beginning of something sustainable—with characters who'd become people worthy of the happiness they'd found, who'd learned to nurture what they'd built, who understood that love was a daily practice rather than a destination.

Outside the ice cream shop window, Sweetgum settled into its evening rhythms. Lights came on in familiar storefronts, families walked home from dinner or errands, the community she'd chosen as home continued its quiet work of supporting the people who'd chosen to be part of it.

This was her life now—not the one she'd planned or expected, but the one she'd built through patience and courage and the willingness to keep learning. It was better than anything she could have imagined eighteen months ago, when all she'd wanted was to help her son stand a little straighter and worry a little less.

Some doors, once opened, led to rooms you never wanted to leave. The dojo had been that kind of door. This community had been that kind of room. This family—chosen and earned and tended with daily care—was that kind of home.

"Ready?" Khadir asked as they finished their ice cream and prepared to head home.

"Ready," she said, and meant it in every possible way.

AUTHOR'S NOTE

Thank you so much for reading Guarded Hearts, the twelfth book in the Sweetgum Meadows Romance series of stand-alone novels. I really hope you loved it! If you enjoyed this book, please consider leaving a review so that others may also find it. Also, if you haven't read the first books yet, check them out today! Although these are stand-alone novels, the stories all intertwine and progress.

I look forward to introducing you to the other characters in this lovely, family-oriented town where each couple will find their happily ever after.

Would you like to receive bonus scenes and keep up with what's next with my upcoming books? Then, make sure you sign up for my mailing list on my website by visiting ImaniPrice.com.

My full audiobook catalog is available for FREE on YouTube. Check it out here: https://swiy.co/Sweetgum

ALSO BY IMANI PRICE

Book 1: Love Between Us

Book 2: Sweet Sunsets

Book 3: Infinite Kiss

Book 4: Dance With Me

Book 5: In Charge

Book 6: Forever With You

Book 7: Secret Sweethearts

Book 8: Endless Love

Book 9: The Harder We Fall

Book 10: Reservations of the Heart

Book 11: Play by Play

Book 12: Guarded Hearts

Book 13: Healing Hearts

Book 14: Dear Sweetgum

Book 15: Lanterns of the Meadows (novella)

Book 16: Drawn to You

Book 17: Under the Sweetgum Tree

Sweetgum Meadows' Visitor's Guide

To all my lovely readers,

www.ingramcontent.com/pod-product-compliance
Lightning Source LLC
Chambersburg PA
CBHW030139010826
48973CB00002B/630